A Rainstorm
In the Kitchen!

Irene and Joe set the machine on a stool in the kitchen and aimed the nozzles.

"Okay," Danny said. "Throw the switch, Irene."

Rather nervously, she did so. The two pale-bluish rays focused on a spot above the soup pot on the stove.

Suddenly from both Irene and Joe there burst wild cries.

Danny froze.

Over the soup kettle a cloud was forming. Its top was piled into anvil-shaped thunder-heads; below, it was dark gray.

"What—?" Danny choked.

The cloud boiled up, grew thicker and darker. From it came a tiny rumble of thunder. A little bolt of lightning lanced down from the cloud and struck the soup kettle with a hiss. Then, suddenly, it began to rain furiously over the stove. . . .

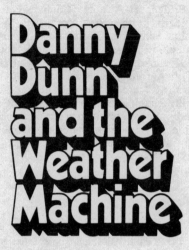

Danny Dunn and the Weather Machine

Jay Williams and
Raymond Abrashkin

Illustrated by Ezra Jack Keats

AN ARCHWAY PAPERBACK
Published by POCKET BOOKS • NEW YORK

Acknowledgments

We are deeply grateful to Nathan Barrey, meteorologist at Bridgeport Airport (Conn.); Patrick Walsh, meteorologist in the New York City Weather Bureau; Julius Schwartz, Consultant in Science, Bureau of Curriculum Research, New York City Schools; Stanley Koencko, president of the Danbury (Conn.) School of Aeronautics; and Louis Huyber, all of whom assisted greatly in the preparation of this book, with technical advice and information.

We are also grateful to Herman Schneider for permission to describe materials from his book *Everyday Weather and How It Works* (McGraw-Hill, 1951).

An Archway Paperback published by
POCKET BOOKS, a Simon & Schuster division of
GULF & WESTERN CORPORATION
1230 Avenue of the Americas, New York, N.Y. 10020

This book is for Michele, Michael,
Timmy and Brett

Contents

1
Something from the Sky

Two boys and a pretty girl, wearing swimming suits and with towels around their necks, stood in the shade of the woods. The blazing August sunlight was filtered and broken by the leaves which hung limp and dusty overhead.

"Gee, it's dry," said Irene Miller, shaking her glossy, brown pony-tail out of the way. "If we don't get some rain pretty soon, there'll be nothing left of the whole countryside."

The taller of the two boys, Joe Pearson, thin and dark, with a perpetually gloomy expression, glanced past her. "Oh-oh," he said. "Danny's got that look on his face again. Whenever he looks like that, it means trouble."

Red-haired Danny Dunn was staring into

1

space. His blue eyes were glazed, and there was a strange smile on his freckled face.

Joe went up close to him. "Danny!" he said. "Snap out of it. The last time you got that look on your face, you tried to make a jet plane out of a fire extinguisher."

"It worked, didn't it?" Danny replied, in a faraway voice.

"Yes, it worked," said Irene. "And it went right through Mr. Winkle's living-room window and wrecked his television set."

Danny shook himself. "This idea is nothing like that one," he said, grinning at his friends. "I was just thinking of a way to prevent forest fires in dry weather. We could pipe water into hollow trees and rig up an automatic sprinkling system that would go into action as soon as a fire started."

Joe grunted. "Where would you get the water from? We've been having a drought—remember?"

"Don't bother him with details," said Irene. "He just makes up theories."

Danny ran his fingers through his hair. "Trees store water in their roots," he said. "We could get it from there, maybe."

"Well, okay," mumbled Joe, beginning to walk on. "Just as long as you don't take it from the swimming hole. In this heat, that's all I've got to comfort me. And we haven't had a swim in days.''

Danny and Irene followed him along the path. Irene said, ''Gee, Danny, maybe your idea would work. Why don't you talk it over with Professor Bullfinch?''

Danny's mother, whose husband had died when the boy was very young, was housekeeper for Professor Euclid Bullfinch, a noted physicist and inventor. A great affection had grown up between the boy and the kindly, quiet scientist, almost like that of father and son, and Professor Bullfinch had taught Danny a great deal about science.

''Well, I don't know,'' Danny replied. ''I hate to bother him these days. He's been working on a new type of power transmitter, and he's been in the laboratory fifteen hours a day.''

The trees ended at the edge of a clearing. In its center was a small, round pond, on the banks of which the young people had built a bench and a rough diving board.

Joe dropped his towel. ''Wow!'' he yelled. ''Last one in is a rotten egg!''

He dashed forward. He ran out on the diving board and leaped into the pond.

''That's funny,'' said Danny. ''Did you hear that?''

"You mean that plopping sound?" Irene said.

"Exactly."

"What about it?"

"No splash," said Danny.

He and Irene stared at each other. Then they ran to the edge of the pond. As they reached it, Joe stood up. There was no water in the pond at all, only soft, sticky mud which covered all the front of him. He wiped his face and glared up at Dan.

"You did it!" he howled. "You and your water pipes in trees."

He stumbled to the side, and Danny and Irene helped him climb out.

"Don't be silly, Joe," said Irene. "The water has just evaporated. It's the heat, and the lack of rain."

Joe looked ruefully down at himself. "Oh, gosh," he said. "Mom will be wild."

"Why? You couldn't help it," Danny said. "And maybe she can plant things on you."

"It's no joke. You know about the water rationing—everybody's supposed to save water. So I promised I wouldn't get dirty."

The other two looked serious. Then Danny said, "I've got it! We're not far from the reservoir. We can go home that way."

"But swimming's not allowed in the reservoir," Joe protested.

"Who said anything about swimming?" Danny said. "We can dip up a handful of water and wash you off."

"It'll take more than a handful," said Joe, wiping feebly at his chest.

"Well, say half a dozen, then."

"But, Danny," Irene protested, "would that be right—taking water from the public reservoir?"

"Why not? The reservoir belongs to the whole town, and we're part of the town, aren't we? And I'll tell you what," Danny added.

"Just to make it fair—when I get home, I won't wash before dinner. That'll save whatever water we use for Joe. There's no sacrifice I wouldn't make for my friend."

"Yeah," said Joe gloomily. "Thanks."

The reservoir was near the town line, about half a mile through the woods. When they came out on the sloping banks, planted with tall pine trees in regular rows, they could see how low the water was: the rocky island in the center stuck far above the surface, and all around the shore the line of the usual water level was clear and dark, like the ring around a bathtub.

Danny led his friends to a sloping shelf of rock that thrust out into the water. "We can dip up a little from here," he said.

"Good!" Irene exclaimed. "It's sunny right here, so the water we'll use would have evaporated anyhow." And she winked at Dan.

But Joe took her seriously. "Say, that's a great idea," he said. "Now you can wash after all, Danny."

Danny did not reply. He was staring upward, shading his eyes with one arm.

"Look at that," he said.

The other two followed his gaze. Something was shining in the sky, something silvery like a half-moon tipped upside down.

"It's a parachute," Danny said, after a moment.

"A paratrooper?" Irene suggested. "No, it's too small."

"Maybe it's a paratrooper from a flying saucer," said Joe. "Let's go home."

"Oh, wait a minute," said Danny. "It could be the nose cone of a missile, or—or something interesting like that."

"Interesting missiles give me goose pimples," grumbled Joe. Nevertheless, he waited.

Lower and lower the thing floated. Now they could see clearly that it was, indeed, a small pale-blue parachute with a box of some sort attached to it.

Suddenly Danny said, "Maybe it's a bomb."

Joe and Irene drew nearer to him. The thing was dropping straight into the reservoir.

"Watch out!" Danny said nervously. "It may blow up when it hits."

Before they could move, the box touched the water and the parachute slowly folded about it like a crumpled sail.

2
The Weather Forecaster

For a long, breathless moment the three waited. Nothing happened. Then Danny said, "If it is a bomb, it's wet by now and that will stop it from exploding."

"Not if it's an underwater bomb," Joe said.

"I don't believe it's a bomb at all," Irene said stoutly. "We didn't hear any plane. And why would anyone drop a bomb that size on a parachute? I'll bet it only came from a flying saucer, or from outer space."

At these words, Danny's eyes widened. "Hey, maybe you're right," he said. "We ought to fish it out of the reservoir. It—it might have germs on it from another planet. It might poison the whole town."

"How can we get to it?" Irene asked, frowning.

Joe looked about. His eye fell on a long, dead branch that had blown down from one of the pine trees. He got it, and went out to the edge of the rocks.

"Danny, you hold my hand," he said. "I'll reach out and try to catch hold of the parachute."

Danny took his friend's hand, and Joe leaned far out with the stick. The parachute was just out of his reach. Further and further he stretched, and suddenly his hand slipped out of Danny's. With a splash, he went headfirst into the water.

Irene uttered a shriek. Danny fell over backward on the rocks. Gasping and blowing, Joe came to the surface and shook the water out of his eyes.

"Oh, well," he said. "Now I'm in, I might as well swim out and get the thing."

A few strokes took him to the parachute. Using his branch, he hooked it up gingerly and brought it to shore. Danny took it from him, and Irene helped him up to the rocks.

"Anyway," he said, wiping his face, "I'm clean."

Danny was already examining their catch.

They could see now that it was a white cardboard box about the size and shape of a large box of corn flakes, with a tape handle and a ring that held it secured to the parachute.

Joe bent over it. "This weather instrument," he read. "A secret code!"

"You're reading it upside down," Danny said, reversing the box. "Here it is—it's a radiosonde."

"Some kind of radio?" Joe wrinkled his brows.

Danny read the square of printing aloud. " 'This weather instrument, known as a *radiosonde,* was attached to a balloon and sent up by a United States Weather Bureau station. During the observation, while the radiosonde was in the air, it operated as a radio transmitter of the temperature, pressure, and moisture of the air through which it passed. The balloon burst at a height of about sixteen miles and the radiosonde came down on the attached parachute.' "

"Look here," Irene added. "It says it's to be returned to the Weather Bureau so they can use it again."

"Yes. Here are the instructions for mailing it," said Danny thoughtfully. "But listen— we're not far from the weather station. It's over on the airfield, beyond Midston University. We could walk it easy from here. Let's take it back now."

"Gosh," Joe protested. "It's more than a mile."

"Maybe they'll give us a reward," Danny said craftily.

Joe jumped up. "What are we waiting for?" he exclaimed.

Leaving the reservoir behind them, they struck off through the woods, and then across some fields until they came to the campus of Midston University, where Irene's father, Dr. Miller, headed the astronomy department, and Professor Bullfinch occasionally lectured. Taking short cuts, they soon came to the airfield, which lay to the north of the town. A main road, Washington Avenue, ran past it, and a little way from the road were two small white buildings. One contained the waiting room, office, and control tower of the airport. The other bore the sign: U.S. DEPT. OF COMMERCE, WEATHER BUREAU.

Danny knocked at the door. After a moment it opened, and a tall man peered out. He had a round, ruddy face and small, sleepy-looking blue eyes, and his lips were curved in a lopsided but pleasant smile.

"Yes?" he said, blinking at them.

"We've come to return your radiosonde," Danny explained.

"That's very kind of you. Won't you come in?" said the man. He held the door wide, and the three friends filed inside.

The little room was crammed with equipment. A teletype machine clattered away in one corner. A long table was piled with diagrams and papers, and the walls were covered with charts of clouds, weather maps, and a large relief map of the United States. Two windows looked out on the airfield, and a door in one wall stood open, revealing another office, a tiny one in which were a desk and a couple of lockers. Cabinets and instruments were ranged all about the main room, and on a corner of the table a teakettle steamed on an electric hotplate.

"My name is Mr. Elswing," said their host. "I'm the meteorologist in charge here."

Danny introduced himself and his friends, and they all shook hands.

"So this is where you make the weather?" Joe said, looking about. "When are you going to give us some rain?"

Mr. Elswing laughed, a jolly, booming laugh. "My goodness," he said. "That's what comes of people thinking of us as *weathermen*, instead of weather forecasters."

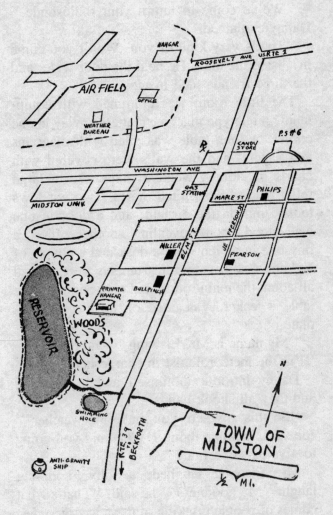

HANGAR

ROOSEVELT AVE. U.S. RTE. 1

AIR FIELD

OFFICE

WEATHER
BUREAU

Rx

CANDY
STORE

P.S #6

WASHINGTON AVE.

GAS
STATION

MIDSTON UNIV.

MAPLE ST

PHILIPS

JEFFERSON ST.

MILLER

ELM ST.

PEARSON

PRIVATE
HANGAR

BULLFINCH

RESERVOIR

WOODS

N

SWIMMING
HOLE

RTE. 39
BECKFORTH

ANTI-GRAVITY
SHIP

TOWN OF
MIDSTON

½ MI.

"Is this machine used for forecasting?" Irene asked, pointing to a tall cabinet with three dials set in its front.

"Yes. That tells the wind direction and wind speed. The top two dials are connected with instruments on the roof of the building. The third dial is a barometer, and gives the air pressure."

Joe was leaning over a long counter on which were a map labeled "Aviation Weather Reporting Stations" and a sheaf of long yellow papers. "Look at this," he said. "This is *really* code!"

"Joe, you've got codes on the brain," Danny grinned.

"Oh, yeah? Well, listen to this," said Joe. "PIREPS VCNTY BDG 1740 R NO TURBC. And I'm not reading upside down, either."

Mr. Elswing nodded. "In a way you're right, Joe. Those are the reports all the stations send in, once every hour. That one is an aviation report." He picked up the paper and read, "Pireps—*pilot reports;* vicinity of BDG— that's the code signal of one of the stations; at 1740—that's five-forty in the afternoon; R— *rain;* No Turbc—*no turbulence,* that is, no high swirling winds."

Joe looked triumphant. "Too bad it wasn't something secret."

"You see," Mr. Elswing explained, "each weather station observes as much as it can about the conditions nearby: the atmospheric pressure, temperature, moisture in the air, wind direction and speed. All these observations are put together to make a large picture of what the weather is like all day long, all over the country. This picture is called a weather map. You can see it in the daily newspapers. Then the meteorologists—that's a better word than weatherman—can make a pretty good guess at what it will be like tomorrow."

"What *will* it be like tomorrow?" Danny asked.

"Dry again, I'm afraid," Mr. Elswing said ruefully.

"Why?" asked Irene. "What's happened to all the rain?"

Mr. Elswing shook his head. "All I can tell you is that we just don't know for certain. The great mass of air that is giving us our weather is staying just about the same. Its pressure is constant, and until, for example, some cold air comes along from the northwest to push it on its way, there isn't much chance of a change."

He sighed, and took some cups from a shelf. "I just wish people wouldn't think it's my fault," he said. "How about a nice cup of tea? I always keep the kettle on. Hot tea seems to cool me off in this kind of weather."

The three young people sat down around the table, and Mr. Elswing, pushing aside the papers, put tea bags in the cups and got down a sugar bowl and a can of milk.

"Why should hot tea cool you off?" Irene demanded.

"Simple," said Danny. "It makes you feel so much hotter that the hot air outside seems cooler."

Mr. Elswing laughed. "Maybe you've got

something there, Dan," he said. "Another reason is that the tea makes you perspire. The moisture on your skin evaporates. When moisture evaporates, it takes heat from surrounding areas, so your skin feels cool."

"Well, it doesn't seem to cool me much," grumbled Joe, who was sitting with his back to the open window. "I'm hot. Even the wind feels hot on my neck."

"Oh, Joe, you're always complaining," said Irene. "Mr. Elswing, tell us some more about what you do in the weather station."

But before the meteorologist could speak, Joe said in a trembling voice, "Danny."

"What?"

"Did you see that horror movie on TV— 'Wolf Man of London'?"

Danny looked at his friend in astonishment.

"Do you remember that guy in the picture who turned into a werewolf?" Joe went on.

"Sure. Why?"

"Because that hot wind I feel—is him, breathing down my neck!"

3
Mr. Elswing Changes

The others sprang up from the table in alarm. A huge, hairy head was peering in through the open window behind Joe. It was tan-and-white, and had mournful brown eyes.

"Why, Joe," Irene cried, "how can you call it a werewolf? It's a cute little puppy!"

They could now see that it was a Saint Bernard dog, standing outside with its chin resting on the window sill. At Irene's words, it seemed to smile, and an immense tail began wagging back and forth so that a real breeze came into the room.

"That's Vanderbilt," Mr. Elswing said. "He's not exactly a puppy, though."

Irene went over and patted the big head. "I

think he's sweet," she said defiantly. "Cute ol' dog. Did the nasty boy call 'um names?"

"Ugh!" Joe said, rolling up his eyes. "Women!"

Danny got up. "You'll have to tear yourself away from that lap dog, Irene," he said. "It's almost suppertime, and we've got a long walk back."

He looked around once more, at the busily chattering teletype, at the instrument dials, the charts and maps and photos of cloud formations. "It must be fun to be a weatherma—er— a meteorologist," he sighed. "Can we come again, Mr. Elswing?"

"Any time you like," said the tall man. "Always glad to have visitors. And if you're really interested, we can always use volunteer observers."

"You mean, to help you here?" Danny asked eagerly.

"To measure rainfall and snow, at your own home, and give us regular reports, which act as a check on our own measurements. Think it over."

"I will," said Danny.

He and his friends shook hands once more with the meteorologist. Then they left the weather station and walked through the gates of the airfield, and down to Washington Ave-

A huge hairy head was peering in.

nue, the wide street that led past Midston University and back to the center of town.

Suddenly Joe said, "Don't you hear a noise like padding feet?"

They stopped. Behind them there was a sound like that of a locomotive chuffing, and the slap of heavy paws on the pavement.

"A footpad," said Joe.

"It's Vanderbilt. He's trailing us like a wolf," Dan said.

"You mean like a whole pack of wolves," Joe said sourly.

"Joe, you stop that," said Irene. "How would you like it if I talked about you that way?" She put her arms around the Saint Bernard's neck. "He just followed us because I said a kind word to him."

"Well, you'd better say a kind good-by to him," Danny put in. "Mr. Elswing's probably looking for him now."

"Go home, Vanderbilt," Irene said, pointing back toward the airfield. "I'll come and visit you again, soon."

The dog did not move. He just stood and looked lovingly at Irene, panting heavily with his tongue hanging out.

"Maybe we could ride him back," Danny suggested. "He's big enough. It'd be easier than walking all that way."

"Shame on you, Danny Dunn," said Irene. "He's more tired than you. Can't you hear him pant? You ought to carry him."

"Oh, no!" Joe burst out. "I quit! Why can't you like canaries, or goldfish, Irene? Why does it have to be dogs?"

"He'll go where Irene goes," Danny said. "Come on. You hold his collar, and we'll take him home."

They marched back to the weather station, and knocked at the door. It opened. Danny, with a smile, began to speak. Then his smile froze.

Mr. Elswing was scowling horribly. With his mouth turned down, his large round face seemed to sag into his neck, and under his beetled brows his small blue eyes were dull and cold.

"What are you doing with that dog?" he snarled, before Danny could say a word. "Let go of him. And get out of here. No visitors!"

He grabbed Vanderbilt by the collar. The dog tucked his tail between his legs and hung his head, and a low, sad whine issued from him. Mr. Elswing dragged him into the weather station and slammed the door.

"G-g-gosh!" Joe stammered. "What happened to him?"

The three, stunned and silent, turned away

and walked back to Washington Avenue. Then Joe said, "I know what it was—split personality—when a man is two people at once."

"Huh?" Danny grunted.

"Sure. I saw it on another TV horror show," said Joe. "There was this good guy, and when the moon was full he turned into a monster—"

"Don't be silly," Danny said. "The moon isn't even out now."

"Is that all you watch on TV, Joe?" Irene asked, pursing up her lips. "Horror movies?"

"Nope." Joe shook his head. "I only watch those before going to bed."

Hmf," Irene sniffed. "Your parents shouldn't allow you to watch such things."

"They don't," Joe grinned.

"Still," said Danny, "something is certainly wrong with Mr. Elswing. Maybe it *is* split personality."

"We'd better not go back there, ever," Irene said firmly. "How do we know what he'll be like next time? He might try to stab us with a weather vane, or something."

They walked on for a moment or two in silence. Then Danny said thoughtfully, "There's no need to go back."

Irene took him by the arm, and turned him to face her.

"You've got something up your sleeve, Dan," she said.

"Up his sleeve? He's not even wearing a shirt," said Joe.

"Come on, out with it," said Irene.

"Okay. Very simple," Danny said at last. "We don't need to go back to *his* weather station. We can build our own!"

4
The Homemade Weather Station

Professor Bullfinch's inventions brought in enough money in royalties so that he could maintain his own laboratory in which to carry on research in many different branches of science. This laboratory was built onto the back of his house, and consisted of a large room in which experiments were conducted, and two smaller alcoves, one containing filing cabinets and reference books, the other crowded with shelves full of supplies.

In this latter alcove, the three friends gathered next morning. They were bent over a number of intricate, small parts which Danny had spread out in front of him on a table.

Joe said with a worried look, "But Danny, are you positive you know how to put it together again? Because my father doesn't know we borrowed his barometer."

Danny picked up a small piece and studied it. "Don't worry," he said. "I'm pretty sure."

"Oh, no!" Joe howled, holding his head. *"Pretty* sure!"

The noise brought Professor Bullfinch into the alcove. "What on earth is the matter?" he asked. "Is someone hurt?"

"Not yet," groaned Joe. "But I will be."

"You know how Joe squawks, Professor," Danny said cheerfully. "We borrowed his father's barometer so I could take it apart to see how it works. We want to build one of our own. Now he's worried that I may not be able to put it together again."

The Professor pushed his glasses up on his forehead. He was a tubby, merry-looking man with rosy cheeks and a bald head across which a few strands of hair were plastered. He said, "Danny, *do* you know how to put together a barometer?"

Danny rubbed his chin. "We-e-ell," he said, "I've never actually done it before. . . ."

"Oooh!" Joe collapsed tragically in a chair. *"Now* he tells me."

"Dear me," said the Professor. "Danny, I'm afraid you acted without thinking, again.

"I'm afraid you acted without thinking again."

I've had occasion to tell you before not to be so headstrong.''

Danny said nothing, and the Professor went on more gently, ''A barometer is relatively simple. But I'm afraid you've broken the airtight seal on the case, and that isn't easy to fix. Also, the hairspring must be coiled tightly, and you haven't the tools with which to do that.''

Danny hung his head, and his cheeks began to burn. ''You're right, Professor Bullfinch,'' he said. ''I—I guess I just thought it was the best way to find out how the thing worked.''

''I'm not saying anything against your scientific curiosity,'' said the Professor. ''But you must think before you act. Why did you want to make a barometer?''

''We were going to set up our own weather station,'' said Irene. ''We looked in the encyclopedia and found that we'd need some basic instruments like a barometer, a rain gauge, a wind vane, an anemometer. . . .''

''Most of those things are easy to make for yourself out of odds and ends,'' said the Professor. He went to a bookshelf at one end of the room, and got down a slim volume. ''Here's a book I got from the author, who is a friend of mine. It's called *Everyday Weather and How It Works,* by Mr. Herman Schneider.''

He flipped it open to a picture. "Here's a simple way to make an anemometer, which is a machine for telling the speed of the wind. You use four paper cups, and fasten them to arms made of cardboard. When the wind blows, it turns the cups. By counting the number of turns in thirty seconds and dividing that number by five, you will get the wind speed in miles per hour. Or you can take it to the weather station and compare it with the one they have there."

Danny glanced quickly at Irene, but neither of them said anything.

The Professor was turning over the pages of the book. "Here's a way of making a weather vane out of a coat hanger and some heavy cardboard cut in the shape of an arrow. Or you can make one out of light wood, and mount it on a post with a nail so that it will turn with the wind. As long as you know where north is, you can figure out the direction from which the wind is blowing."

"What about a rain gauge?" Danny asked.

"Merely a glass jar with a funnel in it to catch the rain. Then you measure how much rain has fallen. You can use my steel ruler, marked in sixty-fourths of an inch."

He paused. "But the barometer is another matter. I'll call Mr. Pearson and explain what happened. But what are *you* going to do about it, Danny?''

''I've got some money saved up,'' Danny said earnestly. ''I'll buy another one for Joe's father just like the one I took to pieces. How can you make one without all these springs and things, Professor?''

''Well,'' said Professor Bullfinch, ''Mr. Schneider has a plan for a very good one in his book. But I used to make them when I was a boy by taking some thin rubber from a balloon and stretching it over the top of a tin can. Stretch it very tight, and tape it down securely. In the center of it, glue a broom straw so that the end of the straw sticks out over the edge of the can. That's your pointer. Glue a piece of cardboard, marked off with lines close together, to one side of the can, so that the straw can move up and down the edge of it. That will be your scale.

''Now, when the air pressure increases, it will push down the rubber sheet, and the end of the straw will be pushed up on the scale. By checking the scale every day, you can tell whether the air pressure is high or low. Low pressure is, of course, associated with stormy weather, and high with fair weather.''

''Let's make one now, Professor,'' Danny said enthusiastically. ''Will you help us?''

Professor Bullfinch took out his watch. "I can help you for a little while," he said, "but I've got to keep an eye on the time. I must catch the one-thirty plane."

He shut his watchcase with a click and stood for a moment rubbing his chin thoughtfully. Then he said, "You can set up your weather station in this alcove. But while I'm away, please be careful of the things in my laboratory."

"Where are you going, Professor?" Danny asked.

"To Washington. My friend, Dr. A. J. Grimes, has invited me to discuss my new engine with the chairman of the Academy of Scientific Research."

"Your new engine?" Danny's eyes opened wide. "Is that the model you've been working on? Can we look at it?"

"Certainly." Professor Bullfinch led the way into the laboratory. On a long, stone-topped bench stood a gray metal cube, about two feet square. On each side were handles, on the back a knife switch, and on the front two long tubes, each shaped something like the nozzle of a garden hose. The Professor patted the top of this device.

"This is my ionic transmitter," he said proudly. "It provides a way of sending electrical energy without wires, by means of two beams of charged particles. Inside this case is a wet-cell battery. When I start the machine, the electrical energy of these batteries can be transmitted to the proper receiver and turned into light and heat—it can be made to light an electric bulb, for instance.''

''That's keen!'' Danny exclaimed. ''Will you show us?''

''Not if you want me to help you with the weather station,'' the Professor replied. ''I haven't time for both. The engine can wait until I get back from Washington, my boy.''

He turned toward the alcove. Then, suddenly, he stopped and swung round. ''Danny,'' he said.

''Yes, Professor?''

''I know how curious you are, and how often you jump into things without thinking carefully of all the consequences.''

''Me?'' Danny said innocently. Then he blushed. ''I guess you're right,'' he said humbly.

''I want you to do something,'' said the Professor.

''Yes, sir?''

''This time, I want you to exercise good judgment and discipline while I'm away. Think twice before you plunge into any—well—any rash ideas.''

Danny sighed. "All right, Professor Bullfinch," he said. "I promise."

"Very well." The Professor, with a cheery smile, rubbed his hands together. "Now, let's get to work. We just have time to make the barometer."

5
"Somebody's Crazy!"

All that afternoon, after the Professor left for
Washington, the three friends worked on the
instruments for their weather station. Irene and
Joe went home limp and exhausted, but eager
for the morning, when they would begin forecasting.

Danny stayed up late that night, reading all
the books he could find, in his own and the
Professor's library, on the subject of weather.
With a flashlight under the tent of his blanket,
he read about cold fronts and warm fronts, humidity, condensation, and precipitation, until
his head was spinning. When at last he fell
asleep, he dreamed that he was struggling
through a hurricane with an enormous barometer chained to his ankles.

Joe and Irene came over shortly after breakfast, and they soon had all their instruments set up and ready. The Professor had loaned them several thermometers, one of which they hung on the inside wall for quick checking of the temperature; the other two were arranged in a box just outside the window, with the bulb of one immersed in water. On the box, Danny had fastened a table of wet-and-dry-bulb readings taken from the Sea Scout Manual of the Boy Scouts. Using this, they could determine the relative humidity—that is, the percentage of water vapor in the air—by comparing the readings on the two thermometers.

They had their homemade barometer on a shelf against one wall, and the other wall was covered with a large map of the United States, on which pins with paper flags on them marked the weather fronts—the front lines where cold and warm masses of air battled. Irene's portable radio stood beneath it, so that they could listen to the daily weather reports. On poles outside, a little way from the window, were the weather vane and the anemometer with its four cups slowly turning in the early morning breeze. Below was the rain gauge, on a wooden bench.

Rubbing his eyes and yawning, Danny took the readings from the thermometers and the barometer. Joe went outside and checked the wind speed and direction, and Irene marked all the information on their map.

"Well, Dan," Joe said, as he came back into the room. "What's the forecast?"

Danny had been leaning out of the window, looking at the sky. With a frown, he said, "Clear, sunny, hot, and dry."

Joe clutched his head. "That's what it's been for the past three weeks!" he cried. "Did we have to go through all this work just to find out that there's no change?"

"Now you know how the weatherman feels," said Mrs. Dunn, Danny's mother. She had come into the laboratory, and now stood just outside the alcove with a tray on which were three glasses of chocolate milk and a plate full of cookies. Her eyes twinkled. "I predict wet whistles and falling appetites," she added, putting the tray on one of the stone-topped lab benches.

"That's the kind of prediction I like," said Joe.

As the three sat down around the bench and went to work on the cookies, Mrs. Dunn, running her fingers through hair as red as Danny's, said, "By the way, Mr. Forecaster, you borrowed my broom yesterday afternoon. May I have it back?"

"Oh, sure, Mom," Danny said. "I'm sorry. We needed a broom straw for our barometer."

"Well, I need a broom straw now, to test a cake I have in the oven," said his mother. "To say nothing of a little sweeping I have to do."

"What kind of a cake will it be, Mrs. Dunn?" Joe asked innocently.

"Chocolate fudge."

Joe's face lighted up. "In that case," he said, "I think maybe Mom would let me stay for dinner."

Mrs. Dunn laughed. "All right, you've talked me into it," she said. "You stay, too, Irene. I'll phone Joe's mother and run next

door to ask yours. And by the way, Danny, please bring back the plate and glasses. I hope you won't need them for rain gauges, or anything.''

''No, Mom. We won't.''

When Mrs. Dunn left with her broom, the three friends finished the cookies and milk. Danny turned his glass upside down over his mouth to catch the last drops. He put the glass on the bench, and a pensive look came over his face.

At the other end of the bench stood the Professor's new machine.

Irene picked up the three glasses and put them on the tray. As she took Danny's glass, she saw the look in his eyes and followed the direction of his gaze. "Don't do it," she said warningly.

Danny raised his eyebrows. "Do what?"

"You've got one of those sudden ideas of yours. Didn't the Professor tell you to think twice before you plunged into anything?"

Danny nodded. "One . . . two . . . ," he said. Then his expression changed. "You're right. I'm going to stay out of trouble this time. I hereby resolve not to touch the Professor's machine while he's away. There!"

Danny tapped his fingertips together, and sighed. "All the same," he said, "I wonder how it works. Joe . . . why don't you turn it on, and let's see what happens?"

"Me?" Joe sat up straight. "Why me?"

"Well, if I touch it, as Irene says, there's likely to be trouble because I won't be able to stop. But look—the nozzles are pointing toward that electric light near the wall. If you close the switch on the back of the machine, we'll see whether the light goes on or not."

"Suppose the thing bites me?" Joe grumbled. "Anyway, it's day. Who needs a light?"

"Don't be silly, Joe. Go ahead. Aren't you interested in a new and exciting invention?"

"I don't think so," Joe said doubtfully. "Am I?"

"All you have to do is close the switch and see if anything happens. Then we'll open it again."

Joe advanced cautiously on the machine. Stretching out one hand, very gingerly, he pushed the knife switch shut.

"Did anything happen?" he asked. He had his eyes tight closed.

"Nope," said Danny in a disappointed voice. "The light didn't go on. Nothing happened at all, as far as I can see."

"It's just as well," said Irene. She went into the alcove. "Let's get back to the weather station. If the machine had worked, heaven knows what you'd have wanted to do next."

"She's right," Joe said. "We really shouldn't fool with it, Dan. Something might go wrong."

"Don't talk like a goon," said Danny, kicking his heels sulkily against the rungs of his stool. "How could anything go wrong by just turning it on? And we're not fooling with it, we're experimenting. Gosh, the Professor lets me experiment with *all* his materials, and use any of his apparatus or his inventions as long as I'm careful. He knows I'm a scientist, too. Why, if he were here—"

He broke off, and jumped to his feet. From the other room came Irene's voice, shrill with excitement.

"Danny!" she called. "Come here, quick!"

He rushed to the alcove with Joe at his heels. Irene pointed to the thermometer that hung on the inside wall.

"Look," she said. "What is it registering?"

He bent over and peered at it. Then he stood up, openmouthed. "It says ten below zero," he stammered.

"That's right," she said. "Ten below zero—but the air feels just as warm to me as ever."

"The thermometer is crazy," said Danny.

"Somebody's crazy," Joe said. "Hm. . . . Maybe it's us."

6
Trouble in
the Kitchen

After a moment, Danny reached out and touched the wall.

"It's cold," he said in astonishment.

Joe nodded. "Then there's nothing wrong with the thermometer," he said. "So it *must* be us."

Danny was feeling all over the surface of the plaster wall. "Water pipes?" he muttered. "No, too cold for that. It seems to be concentrated in a kind of circle right around the thermometer."

"Maybe it's something on the other side of the wall," Irene said. She darted into the laboratory.

Danny and Joe followed her. Irene stopped

so abruptly that they bumped into her. "Look at that," she said in a whisper.

On the wall of the laboratory there was a circular patch of something that gleamed like silvery glass.

"Ice!" Danny cried.

"Great jingle bells!" said Joe. "Something tells me our forecast was cockeyed. The weather *is* changing."

"It's not the weather, Joe," Danny said. He walked close to the ice patch, put his hands on his knees, and carefully sighted back from it at the Professor's machine. "Pointing right at it," he said with satisfaction.

"You mean it's that machine that's doing it?" said Joe.

"Yes. We never turned it off."

"But I thought it wasn't working," said Irene.

"It is, though. See here," Danny said, beckoning to her. "Stand where I am, and bend over, and you can see that there are two faint rays of light coming from the nozzles. They meet right here, at this place where the ice has formed. They were too faint for us to spot before, from where we were sitting."

Irene and Joe stared at the rays, and then at the icy circle on the wall. "Gosh!" Joe breathed. "A cold ray!"

"Right," said Danny. "Somehow, the ray is making that patch of wall cold. Moisture is condensing out of the air and freezing. Look here—" He pointed to a basin against the wall, with a water faucet for rinsing out chemical apparatus. "The faucet's leaking a little, and that, plus the warmth in here, is making the air damp enough at this spot for the ray to condense moisture out on the wall."

"I see," said Irene. "It's like when you pour ice-cold water into a glass. The outside of the glass gets steamy, and that's the moisture being condensed out of the air by the chill of the ice water."

Danny nodded absent-mindedly. "Ice water?" he mumbled.

"Oh-oh," said Joe, backing away. "I feel trouble coming. Look at his face, Irene. He's got that glazed look."

"This isn't trouble." Danny grinned. "It's refreshment."

"It is? Well, go on, then."

"Suppose we had a pitcher of lemonade, and we beamed the ray at it?"

"Lemon ice!" Irene said.

"Sure. It would be a quick freeze." Danny looked from one to the other. "What do you say? Shall we try it?"

"Well," Joe said slowly, "it doesn't really

sound as though anything can go wrong with that. Okay. I'm game.''

"What about your resolution not to touch the machine?'' Irene asked, with her hands on her hips.

"Hmmm,'' Danny said. "Well, I *won't* touch it. You and Joe pick it up and carry it.''

She sighed. "Danny Dunn,'' she began.

Danny interrupted. "Don't you see? That way I won't be tempted to go any further with wild ideas.''

"Mmhmm,'' said Irene.

"You two bring it along into the kitchen,'' Danny said. "I'll start making lemonade.''

Mrs. Dunn was not in the kitchen when Danny entered. She had gone next door to ask Mrs. Miller, Irene's mother, if Irene could stay for dinner. A pot of soup was simmering on the stove, and Danny sniffed appreciatively at it. Then he got lemons out of the refrigerator, filled a pitcher with lemon juice and water, and stirred in several spoonfuls of sugar.

Irene and Joe came in with the machine. It was small, and not too heavy for them to carry. They set it on a stool, under Danny's direction, and aimed the nozzles at the pitcher of lemonade which stood on the kitchen table.

"Okay,'' Danny said. "Throw the switch, Irene.''

Rather nervously, she did so. In the steamy air of the kitchen, the pale-bluish twin rays could be seen more clearly. They just missed the lemonade pitcher, going over it and focusing on a spot above the soup pot on the stove.

"Hold on," Danny said. "Don't try shifting the machine. I'll just put a couple of cookbooks under the pitcher."

He went to the shelf and got down two books of recipes. He was just about to bring them to the table when from both Irene and Joe there burst simultaneous wild cries:

"Hey!"

"Yipes!"

Danny froze as if the cold ray were hitting him.

Over the soup kettle a cloud was forming, no larger than a sofa cushion but unmistakably a cloud. Its top was piled into anvil-shaped thunderheads; below, it was dark gray.

"What—?" Danny choked.

The cloud boiled up, grew thicker and darker. From it there came a tiny rumble of thunder, like the growl of a small dog, but genuine thunder nevertheless. A little bolt of lightning lanced down from the cloud and struck the soup kettle with a hiss. Then, suddenly, it began to rain furiously over the stove.

The three friends stood staring, unable to

49

move a muscle. The rain filled the soup pot and overflowed its edge. The gas flame went out, and water poured down onto the floor.

Then Danny came to his senses. He sprang to the stove and turned off the gas. "Joe!" he yelled. "Stop the machine! Open the switch! Quick, before we're flooded out!"

"But-but-but," Joe stuttered.

Irene jumped forward and pulled the switch open. The rays vanished. A moment later, the cloud was gone.

"How—?" Irene began.

She got no further. Mrs. Dunn opened the back door and stepped into the kitchen. She stared at the three young people, then at the stove and the great puddle of water on the floor.

"Danny!" she exclaimed. "What on earth are you doing?"

Danny's face was bright crimson. "Gee, Mom," he said, and gulped. "Gee. I'm sorry. We couldn't help it. It—it—it rained in the soup!"

7
Good Old IT

Mrs. Dunn's eyebrows slowly rose. Then she felt Danny's forehead.

"You don't *seem* to have a fever," she murmured.

"I haven't, Mom. It was just that—"

Mrs. Dunn shook her head. "Danny, surely you must realize that experiments belong in the laboratory, not in the kitchen."

"I do, Mom. But we—"

"And look at my soup! Good heavens, surely you're old enough not to play with food? Adding water to soup only thins it. I could have told you that."

"I know, Mom. But I—"

"It's ruined!" Mrs. Dunn began to look angry. "Irene, I'm surprised at you, letting these boys spoil good soup."

"But I didn't—" Irene began.

"And my nice, clean floor, covered with water. Haven't you children any sense? Wasting water in this dry weather!"

"But, Mom!" Danny said. "Honestly, we—"

"Don't you 'honestly' me, young man. And what's this box? A radio? No, don't tell me. Whatever it is, get it out of my kitchen. And you get the mop, Dan, and clean up this mess."

In moments, she had whirled them about, thrust a mop into Danny's hands, a sponge into Irene's, a pail into Joe's. The three friends looked sadly at one another, and began the job of drying the floor and the stove, while Mrs. Dunn, still grumbling crossly, did what she could to salvage the watery soup. When they were all done, and the kitchen was more or less restored to order, Joe and Irene lugged the machine back to the laboratory, with Danny behind them, hugging something to his breast.

"I got away with the pitcher of lemonade," he said, once they were safely in the lab. "It's not cold, but it's comforting."

"I need comfort," Joe groaned. "Oh, my

aching back. I knew there'd be trouble. I warned you, didn't I?''

"Oh, don't be so goopy, Joe," said Irene. "Danny, what did happen? How could that cloud form? Where did all that water come from?"

"Wait a minute," Danny protested. "One question at a time. I think I know how it happened."

Deliberately, he poured some of the warm lemonade into a clean test tube, and drank it down. Joe took another test tube and did the same, saying under his breath, "This is just like that horror movie, 'Grandson of the Werewolf,' where the guy drinks from a test tube and turns into a monster. . . ."

"Go on, Dan," said Irene. "Speak up."

"Well," said Danny, "you remember the Professor said his engine projected beams of charged particles? When I was studying up on weather, one of the theories I read about was that clouds form because water droplets condense around chilled particles."

"Slow down," Joe interrupted. "What kind of particles? I don't get it."

"Oh, for instance, little bits of salt, scooped up from sea spray by the wind and carried high in the air. Or dust, or soot from chimneys, or pollen from plants—all kinds of very tiny specks. These are called *nuclei*. High up in the air, where it's cold, they chill. Then moisture condenses around them out of the air and forms lots of little drops. Millions of 'em all together make a cloud."

He paused, frowning. "I couldn't seem to find a clear statement about what makes a cloud turn into rain," he went on. "In some cases, it seems that the top of a cloud gets very cold. The drops turn to ice and start falling, because they're heavy, and as they fall they gather other drops around them and pretty soon they're all

falling. When they get to the warmer air below, they melt, and they're rain. Maybe that's what happened in the kitchen. Maybe not.''

"What else could have happened?'' Irene demanded.

"You know, the tiny particles projected by the machine were very cold. And the air in the kitchen was full of moisture. Steam was rising from the pot. The cold particles acted like nuclei. Water droplets formed around them and made a cloud. As it rose, and as the cold ray chilled it some more, it began to condense; it couldn't hold all that water, and the water fell out. So it rained in the soup.''

Irene, her elbows on the lab bench and her chin on her palms, stared intently at him. Then she sat up straight. "Why—why—this means we can end the drought!" she cried.

"No," said Danny. "I thought of that. But it's obvious that the machine will only make rain when the air is supersaturated—when it's so full of moisture that it can't hold any more. And the weather now is pretty dry, too dry for us to make a cloud outside. Anyway, I think the machine can only make little clouds, and miniature rainstorms."

Joe had been listening, wide-eyed. He jumped up so suddenly that he almost sent a rack of test tubes crashing to the floor. "Wow!" he yelled. "We're rich!"

"Hey, take it easy," Danny cautioned, grabbing the rack.

"What are you talking about, Joe?" asked Irene.

"Why, don't you see? This thing has a thousand uses around the house!" Joe waved his arms in the air. "A portable, pipeless shower bath—an easy way to wash dishes—a million uses!"

"Maybe he's right, for once," said Danny. "If the air was damp enough, you could use it to sprinkle the lawn."

"That's right. And it could be used for

washing your car," said Irene. "Or to sprinkle clothes for ironing. Or to fill up wading pools."

"I wonder if the Professor realizes what the machine can do?" said Danny.

"If he doesn't, he soon will," Joe said. "Just call me Joseph Pearson, Boy Financial Wizard. As soon as he gets back, we'll tell him about it. I can see it now—Pearson, Dunn, and Miller: Home Rainstorms. Oh—and Bullfinch, I guess."

Danny laughed. He raised his hand, then held it motionless in the air.

"Oh, Joe," he said. "Do me a favor."

"Sure. What?"

"Pat the machine for me, will you? I want to keep my resolution not to touch it."

"Okay," said Joe. "By the way, what did the Professor call this thing?"

"An ionic transmitter."

"That's too long. Let's shorten it to I.T." And Joe leaned over and solemnly patted the metal case. "Good old IT," he chuckled.

8
An Eye
for an Eye

Hopkins' Drugstore was a favorite meeting place of the three friends—when they had any money. On the afternoon following the rainstorm in the kitchen, Irene and Danny sat at the soda fountain waiting for Joe, who had a dollar, a windfall from a visiting uncle. Danny had just changed his mind for the third time and decided to have a triple mint fudge marshmallow banana bonanza, when he became aware of a warm breath on his cheek.

"Cut it out, Joe," he began and, turning, saw a pair of large, sad, brown eyes peering into his own.

"Vanderbilt!" he exclaimed.

At the same time, a deep voice said, "Well,

well, this is a surprise. Danny Dunn, isn't it? And Irene Miller?''

The two cringed away, uncertain whether to run for the door or wait it out. Mr. Elswing, however, looking perfectly friendly and jolly, seemed to notice nothing wrong.

He sat down on one of the stools, and Vanderbilt padded heavily round to Irene and put his chin on her arm.

''Sweet little pup,'' she murmured, patting him. The big dog smiled foolishly, rolled up his eyes, and sank down to the floor where he lay panting.

''Why haven't you come to the weather station to visit me?'' Mr. Elswing asked. ''I've been expecting you.''

Danny relaxed a little. He had been quietly unscrewing the top of the pepper shaker, planning, if Mr. Elswing made any sudden moves, to dip a soda straw in the shaker and, using it as a blowgun, pepper the weatherman with pepper. But Mr. Elswing seemed so normal that Danny put down his weapon and began to breathe again.

''We—we've got our own weather station now,'' Dan said.

''That's fine,'' Mr. Elswing beamed. ''Maybe you can give people better forecasts than I can. Nobody seems to like me these days, just because I have to keep telling them that the weather will be dry and hot.''

"We know," Irene said. "Our own forecast this morning was for fair weather.''

"Yes? I hope people don't start blaming you the way they blame me. You'd think I was responsible." Mr. Elswing rubbed his chin. "I'm in the same boat with everyone else. I've had to save water, and use it carefully.''

He bent forward confidingly. "Maybe you notice how bristly my chin is? I've been shaving only twice a week, and using the water I save that way for my tea.''

"Tea?" Danny snorted, and shrugged. "We've solved that problem. You can drink all the tea you like.''

"What? How's that?''

"Why, with our new rainstorm ray you can condense the steam from your teakettle and use it over again for the next cup of tea.''

There was a long moment of stunned silence. Then Irene burst out, "Oh, *Danny!* How could you?''

Mr. Elswing had a most peculiar look on his face. He opened his mouth as if to say something, and shut it again.

Danny bit his lip. Then he said, "Gosh, I didn't mean to let that out. The ray is still a secret.''

"Well, I—" Mr. Elswing began. "The ray, eh?" He cleared his throat to cover a smile of disbelief, and went on, "I won't say a word to anyone."

"Will you promise?" Danny said earnestly.

The meteorologist nodded and raised his right hand. "I give you my most solemn promise that I won't breathe a word about your— what did you call it?"

"Well, we haven't any actual name for it yet. Joe calls it IT."

"All right. You have my promise, whatever its name is." Mr. Elswing glanced at the clock above the soda counter. "I must run. I just happened to see you through the window, and thought I'd say hello."

He clucked to Vanderbilt, who rose up ponderously and gave Irene a farewell look and a longing sigh. "Bring your machine around to the weather station tomorrow," he added. "It sounds as though it has possibilities. We'll keep it secret, but anything that can give me all the tea I want is worth studying. And I like to encourage young amateur scientists."

He waved gaily to them, and went off with Vanderbilt at his heels. Danny looked after them with a sullen frown.

"What's the matter?" said Irene. "I think

he'll really keep his promise. Is that what you're worried about? He may be a little touched, but he looks honest.''

'' 'Tisn't that,'' said Danny. ''It's what he called me: *amateur!*''

He rested his chin gloomily on both hands. ''What does he think I am, some kid in first grade? And you know what?''

''What?''

''I got the feeling that he didn't really believe me. About the ray, I mean.''

''Well, if he didn't, so much the better,'' said Irene comfortingly. ''That's the best way to keep it secret, isn't it?''

''I guess so,'' said Danny. ''But it's very insulting to me.''

''What's insulting?'' Joe had just come in, and he slid onto the stool next to Danny's. ''Something more insulting than what I've got?''

He grinned, but it was a crooked grin. One of his eyes was puffy, and the skin around it was already turning the rich colors of an autumn sunset.

''Golly! What happened to you?'' Danny asked.

Irene leaned over, looking troubled. ''Does it hurt?''

"Only when I look through it," said Joe wryly. "It was a present from Snitcher Philips."

Eddie Philips was a stocky, broad-shouldered boy who was known to his schoolmates as "Snitcher" because of his bad habit of telling on other people.

"I met him on the corner of Jefferson Street," Joe continued, gingerly touching his eye with one finger. "I don't know why he got so mad. All I said was, 'Good morning, Eddie.' "

"Is that all?" said Danny in surprise.

"Sure, that's all." Joe waved to the counterman. "Let's order. I guess I'll have a hot fudge sundae for me, and a piece of ice for my eye."

They got their ice cream, and Irene kindly gave Joe the cherry from the top of her sundae, while Danny gave him a piece of banana from his. Joe cheered up and began to eat.

"Seems kind of funny that he should punch you in the eye just for saying hello," Irene said, spooning up caramel sauce.

"Oh, he was in a bad mood. I said, 'Good morning,' and then I asked where he was going. He said he was going to visit an uncle of his who works at the weather station."

"Mr. Elswing? His uncle?"

"It was a present from Snitcher Philips."

"Yep. So then I said, 'Oh, you mean that nut? No wonder he has a split personality.' And then he said, 'You keep your trap shut or I'll split *your* personality.' And I said something like 'What do you do at the weather station, Snitcher? Do you snitch on what the weather's going to be?' And we went on and exchanged a few more friendly jokes that way, and all of a sudden he hit me.''

"Oh, I see," said Irene with a grin.

"Maybe he got irritated when I said we were going to have a medal made for him with a big open mouth on it. How did I know he had no sense of humor?" Joe dug up a huge spoonful of ice cream and swallowed it. "But I found out," he added.

Danny stirred the remains of his banana bonanza, and shook his head. "Snitcher's getting to be more of a bully every day. Somebody ought to teach him a lesson."

"Sure. But not me," said Joe. "I don't like to teach anybody who hits so hard."

"No, not you—not alone." Danny put down his spoon. "But listen—do you want to get even with Snitcher?"

" 'Course I do. But—"

"You've heard that old saying, 'an eye for an eye'?"

"Ha! You'd never get close enough to

Snitcher to hit him in the eye."

"That's not what I mean," Danny said mysteriously. "I've got a great idea." He jumped down from his stool. "Come on."

"You mean, we'll all gang up on him?" said Joe. "I don't think that will—"

"Just relax," Danny said. "Follow me. Have I ever steered you wrong?"

"Yes," said Joe glumly.

9
"You May Fire
When Ready. . . ."

The three friends cautiously approached the rear of the weather station from the cover of a clump of raspberry bushes. Behind him, Joe pulled IT, set on a little four-wheeled wagon, a relic of his younger days.

Danny put a finger to his lips. "Do you understand the plan?" he whispered. "Any last-minute questions?"

The others shook their heads.

"Okay. Synchronize your watches."

"Roger," Irene whispered. Joe was silent.

"Well, Joe?" Danny said softly.

"I haven't got a watch," said Joe. "I don't even know what time it is."

Danny scowled at him. "Sh!" he said. "Let's go."

Softly they edged forward until they were only a couple of dozen yards from the side of the building. Then Danny dropped to his stomach in the tall grass. Motioning the others to wait, he wormed ahead, working his way from the back of the building to the side. Holding his breath, he got into the shelter of a large rock, and raised his head. Then he chuckled softly in satisfaction.

He was facing that same large window through which Joe had first seen the dog, Vanderbilt. Inside, Snitcher bent over the long table, on which the teakettle steamed as usual. He was carving his initials in the table top with his pocketknife.

"Aha," Danny said to himself. "So he's alone. His uncle would never stand for that. And the teakettle's on. Here goes the second Boston Tea Party."

He inched back to his friends. Carefully they pulled the wagon up behind the rock, and Joe propped up the front of IT with flat stones so that the nozzles pointed at the window. Irene stood behind them, judging the elevations and whispering directions.

When all was ready, Danny sighted along the nozzles. Then he whispered into Joe's ear, "You may fire when ready, Gridley." Joe closed the switch.

For a long moment, nothing happened. Then, slowly, above Snitcher's head, a cloud began to form. At first, it looked like nothing more than heavy steam from the kettle. Then it thickened, grew darker and more substantial, and began piling into thunderheads. Snitcher, still carving away at the table top, stirred and glanced uneasily around. A rumble of thunder came that even the three watchers could hear. Snitcher looked out the window at the clear sky, with a puzzled expression.

A few drops must have fallen on his head, for he suddenly stared upward. He stood gaping in astonishment. A little bolt of lightning, about a foot long, shot down. It hit him directly on the top of the head, and knocked him sprawling. At the same instant, a furious rainstorm poured down on him. In moments, he and the floor directly around him were drenched.

Irene had jumped to the top of the rock to see better, and she stood with both hands clapped over her mouth, strangling with laughter. From her vantage point, she could see Snitcher lying on the floor with the rain beating on him. He was making wild motions with his hands, as if trying to chase away the cloud. She saw Vanderbilt, who had evidently been lying down in a corner, come over to Snitcher

73

It hit him directly on the head.

and begin licking his face. Snitcher pushed him away, and got to his feet. Then, red-faced and dripping, he kicked the dog.

Irene gasped. At the top of her voice, she shouted, "You leave that puppy alone, you big bully!"

Snitcher went to the window. "So it's you!" he howled, as Danny rose up to stand beside Irene. "I might have known!"

"Dry up, Snitch!" Joe called, getting up also.

"Need an umbrella?" Danny asked.

Snitcher gurgled with fury. Then, finding his voice, he said, "I'll fix you, all of you. Vanderbilt—fetch!"

Vanderbilt put his immense paws on the window sill and heaved himself through the window. He bounded to Irene, and paused long enough to give her face a tremendous lick. She lost her balance and fell flat. Then, seizing the handle of the wagon in his mouth, Vanderbilt began to drag the whole thing away.

Joe grabbed for the machine. He caught it by one handle. It toppled from the wagon. Danny, in the heat of the moment, forgot his promise to himself and fell on it. Vanderbilt went galumphing away with the wagon trailing behind him in the air like a banner.

Snitcher was yelling, "Uncle! Uncle!"

"Ha!" said Joe, with satisfaction. "We made him say *uncle*."

"Not that kind of uncle," Irene gasped, staggering up. In the room, behind Snitcher, they saw the scowling face of Mr. Elswing, dark as a thundercloud itself.

"Quick!" said Danny. "Pick up the machine, you two. Let's get out of here."

Mr. Elswing was shaking his fists. His round face was contorted with anger, and he was roaring something which the very violence of his rage made it impossible to understand.

But the three friends did not wait for a translation. Picking up the machine by the handles, Irene and Joe made off as fast as they could, with Danny right behind them.

10
"What's Wrong with IT?"

That evening, after dinner, Irene came over from next door to visit Danny. The two settled down cosily in their weather-station alcove, with IT on the floor between them and a pitcher of lemonade on the table.

Sipping at a glassful, Irene said, "I wonder if we oughtn't to do something about Mr. Elswing—report him, or something?"

Danny poured himself some more lemonade. "Who could we report him to?" he said. "Who'd believe us?"

"Well, maybe other people know about his split personality. Maybe a doctor would believe us. He might get really violent, you know. It's dangerous."

"Dangerous? You think he'd really—hurt somebody?"

"You never can tell."

"I guess you're right. Maybe we'd better—" The words died on Danny's lips. He gave a violent start. The glass of lemonade leaped from his fingers and broke on the weather machine's metal case. "Glurk!" he said.

"Glurk? What do you mean, glurk?" asked Irene, in annoyance. "Now look what you've done."

Danny gulped like a goldfish and motioned weakly at the doorway.

" 'Glurk' isn't even English," Irene continued. Then she saw what he was doing, and turned toward the door.

"Good evening," said Mr. Elswing quietly.

"G-g-glurk!" said Irene.

The smiling face of Mrs. Dunn appeared behind Mr. Elswing.

"You have a visitor, dear," she said to Danny. "You know Mr. Elswing, don't you?"

Danny nodded, still unable to speak.

"Where are your manners, Dan?" said his mother. "Can't you get up and say hello properly?"

Danny had to try twice before his legs would support him. "H-h-h-h—" was all he could say.

Mr. Elswing was holding Joe's wagon. "My nephew said that you left this behind you," he explained. "It is yours, isn't it?"

"Yes," said Danny.

Mrs. Dunn frowned, and silently shaped words with her lips.

Danny caught his mother's eyes. "Er—yes, thank you."

Mrs. Dunn smiled again. "I'll leave you then," she said. "I know Danny has lots of questions he wants to ask you, Mr. Elswing. He and Irene have been so interested in the weather lately."

When she had gone, Mr. Elswing said, "I'm sorry we didn't have a chance to chat together today."

Irene and Danny stared at him, and then at each other.

Mr. Elswing, without noticing, went on in a gentle tone, "You know, that was a terrible mess you made in the weather station. And I'm afraid some of the papers and instruments got rather soaked. Eddie told me a fantastic story about how it happened—something about a little rain cloud, and how you struck him with lightning." He chuckled. "Now, I want you to understand that I used to play games like that when I was young, too. I sympathize with you. But really, you mustn't shoot water pistols around the weather station from now on. There are some delicate and expensive instruments there that could be ruined by water."

"But, Mr. Elswing," Danny interrupted. "It's true."

"I beg your pardon? What's true?"

"We—we did strike Sni—Eddie with lightning. And it wasn't water pistols, it was IT."

"It was it? It was what?"

"IT."

"It what? What it?" said Mr. Elswing, looking bewildered.

"He means the ionic transmitter," Irene put in. "The rain-making ray we told you about."

Mr. Elswing's eyebrows slowly rose. "Oh, come, now," he said. "You don't seriously expect me to believe that."

Danny's face took on a determined expression. "I'll prove it," he said. "I'm *not* an amateur. You'll see."

He reached for the machine, but Irene clucked at him. "Okay," he said. "I won't touch it. You drag it out, Irene, and aim it at the sink. I'll turn on the faucet."

As Mr. Elswing watched, Irene first cleaned away the broken glass, and then slid the machine out into the laboratory. Danny twisted the faucet so that a trickle of water began to run into the basin. Irene aimed the machine as

"Now look what you've done."

well as she could and, at a nod from Danny, threw the switch.

"Very interesting," said Mr. Elswing. "What is supposed to happen?"

"Just wait," Danny begged. "You'll see."

A long moment went by, then another. Still, nothing happened.

"Well," said Mr. Elswing kindly, "don't be disappointed. That's the sort of thing that always happened to my inventions when I was a boy."

"But I don't understand," Danny said, clenching his fists. "What's the matter with it?"

"I don't know," Irene said. "It—it really doesn't seem to be working, Dan."

"You'll show it to me another time," Mr. Elswing said. "I'm afraid I've got to run along. Meanwhile, please remember what I said. Don't play with water, or water pistols—or even make-believe rain-makers—in the weather station."

"But—" said Danny.

"I can find my way out. Good night. And do drop in and visit me any time you're in the neighborhood."

With a wide smile and a wave of his hand, Mr. Elswing left them. The two young people looked after him, and then turned to IT.

Danny rubbed his head with both hands. "What's wrong?" he groaned. "Oh, my gosh—what's wrong with IT?"

11
Danny Makes
a Vow . . . Again

"Well," Danny said, sighing wretchedly, "there's only one thing for it. I hate to break my resolution, but I'm going to have to touch the machine."

"Oh, Dan!" said Irene.

"No help for it. I've got to inspect it myself and see if I can find out what happened."

He snapped on a bright work light that hung over one of the lab benches. Then, with a shrug, he took hold of one of the handles of the machine and pulled it close to the bench. Between them, he and Irene lifted it to the stone surface.

"Hm. Switch is okay," Danny muttered, inspecting it. "I thought maybe one of the connections was loose, but the wires are soldered to the terminals. Let's see. . . ."

He pushed the machine around. Then he snapped, "Look!"

"At what?"

"Why, don't you see? One of the nozzles is missing."

Irene stared. Sure enough, one of the twin tubes on the front of the machine was gone. "Why on earth didn't we notice it sooner?" she said.

"It's easy to overlook something like that. We were excited, and rushed, on the way home. And the light isn't very bright in the alcove."

Irene bent forward. "The nozzles screw onto these threaded projections on the front," she said. "It must have been loose, and when Vanderbilt grabbed the wagon and the machine fell over, the nozzle dropped off."

"Then it's somewhere around the weather station," Danny said, straightening up and dusting his hands together. "We ought to go right now and look for it."

He went to one of the windows and threw it open. Irene came and stood next to him. "It's awfully late, Dan," she said.

"Yes. But there's a moon. Couldn't we search by moonlight?"

They leaned on the sill together, looking out at the sky. "It's beginning to cloud up, though," said Irene. "See—there's a big dark cloud coming from the west. And—and, Dan—"

"What?"

"Well . . . maybe there's something to Joe's crazy story about Mr. Elswing and the full moon."

Danny rubbed his nose pensively. "Nah!" he said. "Anyway . . . I don't think so. But I guess nothing can happen to the nozzle during the night. And we *would* find it more easily by daylight."

"First thing in the morning, then," said Irene.

"Yes. First thing. I'll go phone Joe."

Irene closed the window. Through the pane, she cast one more glance at the moon, round and gleaming, with the silvery edge of the big cloud closing in on it.

"When the moon is full, he turns into a monster," she whispered. She shuddered, and turned away quickly. "Joe really shouldn't watch such childish programs," she said.

Danny spent a restless and uncomfortable night, worrying about the Professor's machine, and, when he slept, dreaming of Mr. Elswing turning into a werewolf in the moonlight and gnawing on the dial of a barometer. He awoke feeling as if he hadn't had any rest at all, splashed cold water on his face, dressed carelessly, and went down to breakfast. He was trying so hard to remember the exact spot where the machine had fallen over that he absent-mindedly asked his mother to give him another fried nozzle.

Irene joined him in front of the house, and they walked up to the corner of Washington Avenue, where they met Joe.

"Bad morning to you both," Joe grunted. "More trouble, and more trouble. Now it's clouding over. It'll probably rain and we'll get soaked."

"That wouldn't be so bad, Joe," said Irene. "Everybody's hoping that it *will* rain."

"Sure. Me, too. But not when I'm stumbling around outside that weather station. Suppose Mr. Elswing is in a murderous mood today? I remember a movie in which, whenever the weather changes and a storm is coming up, this fellow turns into a bat—"

"Oh, shut up, Joe!" Irene snapped.

Joe looked surprised, but he shut up. They walked on in a rather moody silence, thinking about Mr. Elswing and wondering whether

"When the moon is full . . ."

they'd find the missing nozzle, and oppressed in spite of themselves by the gray sky after so many weeks of sunshine.

They came, at last, to the weather station and went quietly around to the side. "Here's the rock where we set IT up," said Danny. "But there's no sign of the nozzle."

"Are you sure we lost it here, and not on the way home?" Joe asked. "You'd think it would be shining in the grass."

"I'm not sure of anything," Danny replied. "Vanderbilt may have carried it off somewhere."

"Maybe he thought it was a bone, and buried it," said Joe.

"Tell you what, Joe," Danny said. "You go round to the other side and search, and begin working your way to the back of the building. Irene and I will search here. We'll meet you in the rear. If we can't find it, we'll just have to backtrack."

"All right," Joe agreed. "Only let's keep quiet so Mr. Elswing doesn't hear us."

He left them, and Danny and Irene began combing the ground, moving slowly with bent heads, kicking aside tufts of grass and turning over stones.

"I don't know," Danny said, after five minutes of this. "It's like looking for a needle in a haystack. It could be anywhere. It's just as likely to be a dozen yards away as right here.''

As he said this, he kicked his foot against a stone. There was a *clink!* The stone rolled away, and there lay the nozzle, its gray metal gleaming dully in the daylight.

''Oh, for goodness' sake,'' Irene exclaimed, laughing. ''Wouldn't you know it?'' She picked it up.

''Sh!'' Danny warned, involuntarily glancing at the station.

And there stood Mr. Elswing in the window, with his hands in his pockets.

''Hello, kids,'' he said cheerfully.

Danny was opening his mouth to reply. Suddenly, Joe raced into sight around the edge of the building. ''Run!'' he screamed. ''He's after me!''

Danny and Irene had been tense all morning. This was enough to set them off. Panic descended on them and, without thinking or waiting to ask questions, they turned and fled.

Across Washington Avenue they tore, heedless of the traffic. They ran through the university grounds, dodging students, and galloped into the woods. They crashed through underbrush and brambles, and finally emerged breathless at the edge of the Professor's property.

Danny threw himself on the ground. "I—don't—care," he gasped. "Let him—catch us. I can't—run—any—more."

The other two fell at his side. After a moment or two, when they could breathe again, Danny asked, "By the way, Joe, *who* was chasing us?"

"Why, Mr. Elswing," Joe panted. "I saw him through the window over on my side of the building. He yelled something at me, and started to climb through the window. So I ran."

Danny's jaw dropped. "But he couldn't have," he said. "He was standing on our side, and he smiled and said hello as sweet as pie."

Joe scratched his head. "The pie over on my

side was nothing but crust,'' he said. ''I'm *sure* I saw him.''

''You just thought you did,'' Irene said.

''Maybe it was a double exposure?'' Joe suggested.

''No, you were thinking so much about him, and about those horror movies of yours, that probably what you saw was Vanderbilt looking through the window, and you thought it was Mr. Elswing. You've always been unfair to that poor little pup,'' Irene said.

''Poor little pup!'' Joe rolled over on his back, and moaned. ''Sweet little lap dog! Miniature poodle! Oh, man! I always knew there was something wrong with girls.''

Irene frowned and began to reply. But Danny got to his feet, and said, ''Never mind that. Come on, let's get this nozzle back on the machine. Joe, you put it on. I swear I won't touch it again—and this time I mean it!''

12
The Lemonade Clue

The laboratory in the back of Professor Bull-finch's house had its own private entrance. As the three made their way to it, Mrs. Dunn stuck her head out the kitchen window.

"Hello, wanderers," she called. "Anyone for a little snack?"

"In a few minutes, Mom," Danny answered. "We've got some work to do in the lab, first."

"All right. Oh—Danny."

"Yes, Mom?"

"Don't make a mess in the laboratory. I've just had a wire from Professor Bullfinch. He'll be back tomorrow."

Danny stopped short. "Tomorrow?"

"Yes, he said he might be back in time for

lunch, if he could make an early plane. Isn't that good news?''

''Er—yes. Yes, it sure is,'' Danny stuttered.

He pulled open the laboratory door and fairly flew inside.

''We've got no time to waste,'' he told the others. ''Give Joe the nozzle, Irene.''

She had been carrying it all this time, and now passed it over. With shaking hands, Joe screwed it back in place. Irene aimed the machine at the sink, once again, and told Joe to turn on the faucet. Then she threw the switch.

Nothing happened. There was no sign of the pale beams, no sign of cloud or moisture.

Danny gave a yelp and sank down in a chair.

Irene wrung her hands. ''What'll we do?'' she wailed.

Danny pulled himself together. ''I'll have to break my promise to myself again,'' he said piteously. ''Help me, Joe. Let's get it up on the lab bench.''

Between them, they lifted it to the stone surface. The back plate of the machine was held on by six screws. Danny got a screwdriver and unfastened them. He lifted the plate off.

Inside was a tangle of wires, tubes, and oddly shaped pieces of apparatus. Danny looked at it hopelessly.

''Even if I had seen this before,'' he said,

"I wouldn't be able to figure out what's wrong. We're in trouble."

"I expected it." Joe leaned back against the edge of the sink, and folded his arms. "Now what?"

"It's all my fault," Danny groaned. "I should never have touched it. This is what always happens—I jump into things without thinking, and then—boom! Why don't I ever learn?"

"Aw, take it easy, Dan," Joe said, looking sympathetically at his friend. "Even the Professor said that scientists have to be curious."

"Yes. And curiosity killed this cat—I mean, this machine," said Danny bitterly. "What'll I tell the Professor? Gosh, I don't know. I don't know what to do."

He rubbed his face hard, as if that way he could start his ideas percolating. "I'll take another look inside," he said, but without much enthusiasm. He put his hands on the sides of the machine and pushed it straight, so that the work light would shine more directly into it.

Then he said, "Ow!"

"What's the matter?" Irene asked.

"I cut my finger on something." He popped his finger in his mouth. Slowly, a strange expression spread over his face. He removed his finger and stared at it.

"Is it bleeding?" Irene said. "I'll get a bandage."

"Just a second," said Danny.

"What is it?"

"Well, you're not going to believe this, but my blood tastes like lemonade."

"What?" Joe cried.

Irene said, "Oh, I know why. 'Tisn't blood. Don't you remember last night when Mr. Elswing came to visit us? You were so startled, you dropped your glass of lemonade and it spilled all over IT. That's what's on your finger."

Danny was already inspecting the machine's metal case, and mumbling to himself. Then he said, "Aha!"

"Aha?" said Joe. "Is that good or bad?"

"Both." Danny pointed to the side of the case. "This is all smooth metal. I wondered where I could have cut my finger. Now I see— there's a crack in the metal, right here."

"A crack?" said Irene. "Ah—when Vanderbilt grabbed the wagon, and it fell over. Right?"

Danny snapped his fingers. "If the case is cracked, something inside may be broken."

"Here we go again," Joe muttered.

Paying no attention, Danny peered into the maze of machinery. Wires led from the knife switch on the back plate to a six-volt wet-cell battery inside. Danny reached in, and slid the battery out.

"I was right!" he chortled.

Irene bent over to look at the battery. On the top of it were three plastic caps which covered the openings to the battery cells. When these caps were removed, distilled water could be poured into the battery. One of the caps was cracked almost in two.

"You see," Danny went on, "when the case fell off the wagon, it must have hit the rock and cracked. This cap broke at the same time, and the acid spilled out of the cell of the battery. I'll bet you anything, that's why the machine won't work."

"It's worth trying," said Irene. "Is there another battery around?"

"Look on those bottom shelves," Danny directed. "I'll unhook the cables."

He did so, and Irene quickly found another battery and brought it over. Danny fastened the cables to it, and put it back in place. Without bothering to refasten the back plate, he closed the switch.

"There!" said Irene. "The tubes are glowing."

"You're right. We're back in business."

"Now, I wonder—" Irene began.

She was interrupted by a muffled cry from Joe.

He was waving his arms helplessly. The two rays met at his head, and from the neck up he was lost in a thick, white fog.

"Get me out of here!" he yelled. "Where am I?"

Danny opened the switch, and the fog thinned and faded away, leaving Joe's hair wet and his face dripping.

"Welcome back, Chief Rain-in-the-Face," Danny laughed. "Stay away from the sink, from now on."

"Well, it's working, anyway," said Irene. "What about the crack, Dan? How can we fix it?"

"Professor Bullfinch isn't due home until lunchtime, at the earliest," Danny replied. "So tomorrow we'll take the machine to Mr. Krantz, the welder, right after breakfast. He can fix it."

"Yes, and this time we'll tie it down on the wagon," said Joe, mopping his face with his handkerchief. "I'll bring over a roll of wire."

Irene put a hand on Danny's arm. "Dan," she said, "I want to ask you something."

"What?"

"You are going to tell the Professor what happened, aren't you?"

Danny bit his lip. Then he said bravely, "Of course I am. There's no use trying to duck out on it. Maybe when he finds out we can make midget rainstorms with it, he'll forgive me."

But in his heart, Dan knew that the Professor would be disappointed in him for not using self-discipline—and knew, too, that this disappointment would be justified.

13
Mr. Elswing
Really Splits

Mr. Krantz, WELDING, BRAZING & MET-ALWORK CO., was a fat, red-faced man who was continually wheezing, clucking, panting, and chuckling as if he were a kind of engine himself. When the three friends came into the shop, he was welding a seam in a steel tank. He snapped off the torch, pushed up his dark goggles, and surveyed the young people who stood in a row, with IT on the wagon in front of them.

"Well, well, well," he said. "H-t-t-t! Danny Dunn and Company. And who's this other one, the feller on the wagon? Looks familiar."

"We need a little patching done, Mr. Krantz," Danny said.

"Oho! Aha! Another one of your inventions,

hey? I remember the last one. Didn't I make you a clamp so you could hook your telescope on your Ma's piano stool, so you'd have a revolving base for it? So you could follow the stars, hey? And you kept turning and turning it until the top came off the piano stool and down it fell, and I had to repair the telescope too? What is it this time?''

"Nothing like that, Mr. Krantz.'' Danny grinned. "This is just a metal housing for a kind of box that has a crack in it.''

Mr. Krantz put his hands on his knees and bent over. "Just a kind of box, hey? I remember this—I ought to, 'cause I made it myself. It was for the Professor. What's happened to it?''

"It sort of . . . fell over,'' Danny said reluctantly.

"Mmhm. Way, way over. Well, I shouldn't ask too many questions. My business is to weld. Right? Don't touch anything, and leave me alone with this for a few minutes.''

Humming and snorting to himself, Mr. Krantz unfastened the loops of wire with which they had bound IT to the wagon, and lifted the metal case to his workbench. While Dan and his friends watched in silent interest, he put flux on the crack and then took up a brazing rod and his torch. With the torch, he melted brass down into the crack, and in a moment or two had made a smooth, neat line which sealed up the housing and made it as good as new.

"There she is," he said. He put IT back in the wagon, and then picked up the wire. "You don't mind if I fasten it back in place for you? Good. Not like you had it, all messy, but this way—"

He bound the wire two or three times around IT, through the handles and under the wagon. Then he coiled the leftover wire into a large loop and twisted it at the top. "Now," he said, "you've got a kind of extra handle on top. You can hold it to steady the thing, and also to carry it if you have to. That way, you won't be so apt to let it—er—*fall over.*"

He refused to take any pay for the job, saying that it was an honor for him to work for the great inventor, Danny Dunn, and then, gurgling with amusement, he returned to his welding.

The three dragged the wagon down the street. Mr. Krantz's shop was near the Washington Avenue gas station, and when they came to the corner they saw that a great many people were making their way along the avenue toward the airfield.

Danny went into the gas station, where one of the attendants was standing, watching the crowd with his hands in his pockets. "Excuse me, Mr. Collodi," he said, "but what's going on? Is there a fire or something?"

"Nope." Mr. Collodi pushed back his cap with a greasy hand. "They're going to watch the seeding."

"Oh, I see," said Danny. "Thanks a lot."

He started to turn away. Then, "Huh?" he cried. *"What* seeding?"

"The cloud-seeding," said Mr. Collodi. "It's been so dry lately, you know, and now it's been cloudy for a couple of days, I heard a fellow say they're going to scatter some stuff from a plane to make it rain. They call that cloud-seeding. They got a plane from East-bridge, I hear."

Danny swung round to the others. "Let's go watch!" he said.

"You mean, they actually put raindrop seeds up there and hope they'll grow?" Joe asked.

"Don't be silly, Joe," said Irene. "They throw out tiny particles of dry ice, or make silver iodide smoke, so that the moisture in the clouds may condense around the little cold particles. If it does, those cold droplets sometimes begin to fall, and they may collect other drops, and so it rains. It's pretty much like what happens with our machine.''

"Say!" Mr. Collodi put in. "That sounds interesting. Maybe I'll go watch it myself.''

He yelled to another man in the office, "Hey, Gil! Take over, will you?'' Then he said, "Come on, kids. I'll give you a lift. If you're going, you don't want to have to lug that wagon of yours all that distance.''

"Let's go,'' Danny urged. "It won't take more than a few minutes.''

"But suppose the Professor gets home first?'' Irene said. "We ought to take IT back to the lab.''

Danny paused. Then he said, "His telegram said that he'd get home for lunch if he made the early plane. But we've got almost an hour before lunchtime. Come on. We've never seen a cloud-seeding.''

They followed Mr. Collodi to his panel truck, which was parked beside the office, and he boosted the wagon with the machine in it into the back of the truck. The three squeezed into the cab, and Mr. Collodi drove off.

The crowd was growing, and when they got to Midston Airport, Mr. Collodi parked his truck at the gates. The friends thanked him and took their wagon. They pushed their way past the weather station building and then past the airport office. Opposite this the hangar stood, with two or three private planes parked alongside it. Here the crowd had thinned somewhat, and they made their way to the edge of the field, Danny hauling the wagon, while Joe and Irene held the loop of wire to support IT.

Danny approached a tall, thin man who was chewing on a soggy cigar. "Excuse me, mister," he said.

"Yeah?"

"What are they going to seed with—carbon dioxide or silver iodide crystals?"

"With seeds, buddy," said the man shortly. "What else?"

Irene snickered.

The man looked them over with a grin. Then he went on, "Listen, why ask me? I'm only the audience. Go ask the weatherman—out there on the field."

The three turned to follow his pointing finger. Their eyes opened wide, and their mouths fell open in astonishment.

On the field, near the long, dark, shiny, central landing strip, stood *two* Mr. Elswings!

14
IT Takes Flight

"What did I tell you?" blurted Joe. "Split personality!"

Irene rubbed her eyes. The two Mr. Elswings were exactly alike, except that one of them wore a floppy panama hat, and the other carried an umbrella. "It can't be," she said. "Not split personality. That means two people in one body."

"Maybe he split the other way," said Joe. "Two bodies—one people."

"He's twins," Danny said. "Can't you see? They look alike, but one of them has a mouth that turns down and the other is smiling. Let's go out there."

He glanced about hastily. "I'll leave IT right

here," he said, "alongside the wall of the hangar. I'd rather not go running around the field with it. Nobody'll touch it here."

He drew the wagon close to the hangar, and then he and his friends walked out to the twin weathermen.

The Elswings were looking up at the lowering gray clouds. Nearby stood half a dozen other men, all equally intent. Above could be

heard the buzz of a plane's motors. Vanderbilt sat on his haunches near the twins. As the three friends approached, the big dog got up to meet them. Irene patted him and he panted heavily and smiled a greeting.

The scowling Elswing was saying, "It's a

fake, I tell you! The farmers and businessmen who put up the money for this operation have just spent it for nothing."

"Tut, tut, Ralph," said the smiling Elswing. "You're always looking on the dark side of things. The seeding operation may work very well. It depends on a lot of different factors— the temperature of the clouds, the degree of moisture, the wind—you know that. It's a

gamble worth taking, though, isn't it? We do need the rain badly. And if we do nothing, these clouds may simply evaporate and leave us as dry as ever."

"Fiddlesticks, Frank!" Ralph scoffed.

One of the other men, a heavy-set fellow

with a deeply tanned face, put in, "I agree with Frank. We farmers are suffering most. Anything's worth trying, I say."

Another man—he was a local businessman named Roland Glenn—said, "Right. The drought is certainly not good for business. And look at me: I haven't been able to shave properly in days."

"I think you're all crazy," said Ralph Elswing, jamming his hands in his pockets. "My brother Frank is a visionary. If it rains as a result of this seeding nonsense, I'll—I'll eat my new panama hat."

He turned away, and then he saw the three young people. "Ha!" he barked. "Here are some more of your friends, Frank—children!"

Frank beamed at Danny and the others, raising his umbrella in salute. "Why, hello, kids," he said. "Don't mind Ralph. When we used to eat apples, as boys, he always ate the green ones and it made him sour."

Looking from one to the other of the twins, Danny blinked. They had the same round, rather pear-shaped faces, and the same curly hair; they wore the same dark suits and blue neckties. Only their expressions distinguished them. "Gee," Danny said, "am I glad to find out there are two of you. We were worried."

"Didn't you know?" Frank looked surprised. "Why, I thought Eddie, my nephew, would have told you."

"We aren't all that friendly with Snit—with Eddie," said Joe.

"Listen!" Mr. Covey, the farmer, held up his hand for attention. "I think the plane's coming down."

The sound of the motors had grown louder. The men moved back a little way from the strip. In a moment or two, a small blue-and-white airplane dropped from the clouds, swung round in a curve, and then hummed down to make a landing. It rolled to a stop, and two men got out.

The pilot was named Abe Clark. Danny had met him once before, with the Professor. He owned several planes, and ran a small air service, flying freight, dusting and spraying crops, and taking aerial survey photographs. He walked toward the waiting men, pushing back his cap and shaking his head.

"No luck," he said. "I'm afraid conditions aren't right for it."

"Now are you satisfied?" said Ralph, turning to Frank with a short laugh. "You and your umbrella!"

Frank merely smiled. "Are you certain you used enough dry ice?" he said to Clark.

The pilot nodded. "I wish we had been able

to fly our SuperCub. Unfortunately, it's being repaired. This Tri-Pacer is a little more difficult to use for a job like this: it has no tank, for one thing. We have to push the door open to throw out the pellets. But I'm sure we scattered plenty."

"Maybe the particles weren't small enough," suggested Mr. Glenn, the businessman.

"No, I don't think it was that. You know, conditions have to be just right for cloud-seeding, and even then it doesn't always work. The Elswings can tell you about that. We still don't know everything about the weather by a long shot."

"Well," said Frank, "how about trying it just once more?"

"Ridiculous!" Ralph barked.

"I'll try if you say so," said Clark. "Can't tell—it may work."

"Go ahead," said Mr. Covey. "I say, try it again. What about the rest of you?"

The other men, who had all contributed money toward the experiment, nodded. "Okay with me," said one of them.

"We're all agreed," said Mr. Glenn.

Clark pulled his cap down. "All right. Come on, Harve. Let's wind it up again."

They got back into the airplane. Soon the

propeller was turning. They taxied down the strip and turned around.

"We'd better get out of the way," said Mr. Covey. The group moved over to the other side of the strip.

Danny and his friends went along, staying close to Frank Elswing. Irene held Vanderbilt's collar. The big dog paced beside her like a pony. His tongue hung out and he had a pleased simper on his face.

As they all turned round to watch the plane, Danny caught hold of Joe's arm. "Do you see what I see?" he said. "Look over there—by the hangar."

"It's Snitcher," said Joe. "What's he up to?"

Snitcher had edged up close to the hangar wall. He was glancing all around, as if looking for someone. Suddenly he bent down and caught hold of the handle of the wagon. He began to walk toward the back of the hangar, pulling IT along.

"Hey!" Danny shouted. "Drop that!"

"Let's get him!" yelled Joe.

But Irene acted first. She let go of Vanderbilt's collar, pointed to Snitcher, and at the top of her voice cried, "Fetch, Vanderbilt! *Fetch!*"

Vanderbilt uttered a joyous bark. He shot

across the field and seized the back of Snitcher's belt in his teeth. Then he started back, pulling the struggling boy by the belt.

Suddenly everything seemed to happen at once, very rapidly, like a speeded-up motion picture.

As Vanderbilt dragged Snitcher, Snitcher dragged the wagon. The airplane had revved up and had begun to move.

Irene screamed, "Vanderbilt! Hurry!"

Snitcher let go of the wagon. Free of the extra weight, Vanderbilt lumbered across the strip and joined Irene. He stood, holding the howling Snitcher, and wagging his tail so that a cloud of dust arose.

But the wagon, with the Professor's machine on it, stood directly in the path of the rising plane. The pilot either did not see IT—which was not very large—or thought he was above it. But Danny could see that the wheels had not quite cleared the top of the ray machine.

"Oh, no!" he gasped. "It's going to hit." He covered his eyes.

An instant later, Joe tugged at his arm. "Danny—Danny!" he quavered. "Look!"

Fearfully, Danny opened his eyes. The plane was above their heads now. And dangling from one of its wheels, caught by the loop of wire which Mr. Krantz had so carefully made, was the Professor's machine.

15
Beautiful Rain

"Stop that plane!" Danny blurted, quite without thinking how impossible this was.

"What on earth's the matter?" asked Frank Elswing.

Irene, Danny, and Joe all tried to tell him at once. He held up his hands helplessly, and at last cried, "Quiet! For heaven's sake, one at a time."

They fell silent. Then, for the first time, everyone could hear Snitcher's plaintive voice. "Hey, get me loose, will you?" he whined.

They swung round on him. Vanderbilt still had a firm grip on his belt and he was unable to free himself, or even to reach round and hit the dog.

"Let you loose?" Danny repeated. "It's all

your fault. If anything happens to that machine, you'll pay for it."

"What machine?" Frank asked.

"You know," said Danny. "You've seen it. The one I told you about—"

"You mean your invention that makes it possible to condense water out of the atmosphere?" Frank hid a smile, and tried to look grave. "Dear me. That *is* serious."

"What kind of nonsense is this?" said Ralph Elswing.

"It isn't nonsense," said Irene. "And even if it were, Snitcher still had no right to try to steal the machine."

"Snitcher?" Frank looked puzzled.

Before he could go further into the matter, Snitcher blubbered, "Uncle Frank, make Vanderbilt put me down. Stop talking, for gosh sakes, and get me out of this. Uncle Ralph—"

Vanderbilt was looking cheerfully from one to the other, waiting for orders. Irene said, "Poor little puppy. Is 'um getting tired from the weight of Snitcher?"

"Poor little puppy," Joe repeated, with a disgusted air. "Is 'um getting sick from the taste of Snitcher?"

"What is this 'Snitcher' business?" asked Ralph.

"They evidently don't think too highly of Eddie," said Frank in a dry tone. "I can't say I blame them, if he really did try to steal their machine."

"He did," said Danny angrily. "He was trying to get even—"

"I didn't do anything!" Snitcher bawled.

"Oooh! How can you say such a thing?" said Irene.

They all began to talk at once again, arguing, scolding, explaining. In the midst of the noise, there came a loud snapping sound.

Snitcher's belt had broken, and he fell sprawling on the ground. Picking himself up, he ran, holding his pants and weeping with rage and embarrassment, across the field and disappeared behind the hangar.

Vanderbilt uttered a short, quizzical bark, as if to say, "What now?"

"Good boy," said Irene, patting his head. "No, don't kiss me—you'll get me all wet."

"Wet?" Danny repeated. "Hey! I just felt a drop."

There was a sudden, profound silence.

"He's out of his mind," growled Ralph.

"No, he's not," said Mr. Covey, the farmer. "I felt one, too."

They all stared at the soft, heavy gray of the

clouds. The silence spread over the whole airfield, and everywhere people gazed upward.

There was no doubt about it. Fat drops of rain were falling, spattering on the landing strip and puddling the dust. More and more fell, and suddenly it was really raining.

A deep, heartfelt cheer went up from the crowd.

"It worked!" yelled Mr. Covey. "Oh, you

lovely cloud-seeding! It's sprouting! Oh, you beautiful rain!"

Mr. Glenn shouted, "Yippee!" Forgetting his dignity, he tilted his head back to let the drops fall into his mouth.

The president of the bank seized the hands

of the town librarian and danced around with her in the rain. Other people shook hands, cheered, capered about, and laughed. It was as if the whole crowd had abruptly gone mad.

The three young people, although they were happy it was raining at last, were more sensible. When it began to pelt down, they ran across to the hangar and stood just inside. From this vantage point, they watched the excitement

slowly die down as the others also took shelter.

Danny pointed. Out on the field Frank Elswing still stood, grinning and holding up his umbrella. Next to him sat Vanderbilt, with all but his tail under cover. And close by, with the rain streaming from his head, was Ralph Elswing. He was slowly tearing his hat to shreds, scowling furiously, and stuffing the pieces in his mouth.

As the three friends stared, the roar of a plane's engines came to their ears.

"Here comes Mr. Clark," said Irene. "I'll bet he's happy the cloud-seeding worked. I hope he doesn't smash the Professor's machine when he lands."

Danny shook his head miserably. "That's not Mr. Clark. He's flying a Piper Tri-Pacer. What we hear is a twin-engine plane."

He squinted through the downpour. Out of the clouds swooped a silvery passenger plane. It bounced on the runway, and rolled to a stop, turning in toward the hangar. Its door opened and several people got out and ran for the airport office with their coat collars turned up.

But one of the passengers did not run. He looked about at the rain and at the joyful townspeople, and smiled benevolently. He wiped his glasses, and then started for the office at a deliberate walk, as if he were enjoying the warm, delicious summer shower.

It was Professor Bullfinch, home in time for lunch after all.

16
Whatever
Goes Up—

Joe slumped back against the wall. "Danny," he said. "Suddenly I don't feel so good."

Danny was pale. Irene, biting her lip, said, "What shall we do, Dan?"

"That's easy," said Joe. "Let's go home and hide in a closet. And lock the door. And die."

Danny straightened, squaring his shoulders. "There's only one thing to do," he said.

"You mean just die?" said Joe. "And never mind about going home or getting into a closet?"

"No. It'll be my fault if the machine is smashed. I'm going out to tell the Professor."

Danny took a deep breath. He walked out into the rain. After a moment's hesitation, the other two followed him.

He went up to the Professor, swallowed hard, and then said, "Hi, Professor Bullfinch."

"Why, Danny," said the Professor happily, "did you come to meet me? That was very thoughtful of you."

"Yes." Danny's throat seemed to be plugged up. Then he said, "Er—nice weather we're having, isn't it?"

The Professor chuckled. "Now, that's an interesting statement. On the basis of observation, and without detailed research, it would appear that you're wrong because it's raining. But on the other hand, since the rain is so badly needed, perhaps it *is* nice weather after all."

"Yes," said Danny. "Listen, Professor. I wanted to—"

"I know, I know. You're anxious to learn how my meeting with the chairman of the Academy of Scientific Research came out. The results were excellent! I have just time to go home for a bite of lunch, and then I must return to Washington on the first plane I can catch this afternoon. They want to examine my transmitter without delay. Isn't that wonderful?"

Danny simply groaned.

"Dear me," said the Professor, looking worried. "I appreciate your coming to meet me, but perhaps if you don't feel well—"

"Professor Bullfinch," Joe put in, clearing his throat. "On the basis of observation and without detailed research, I would say that we're all getting soaked. Can't we go in where it's dry?"

The Professor nodded. "A practical man is always welcome in the field of science."

Just then, the two Elswings, now both under the umbrella, came by. They had made up their quarrel and they nodded to the Professor, for they both knew him.

"Ah, Frank," said Professor Bullfinch, "it's good to see you. And you, Ralph. Can we go into the weather station with you, and phone for a taxi?"

"Certainly," said Frank. "Come along."

He led them to the weather station. When they got inside and were shaking the rain from their clothing, he turned to his brother with an exclamation of annoyance.

"I do wish you weren't so pessimistic, Ralph," he said. "You were so sure it wouldn't rain that you left the windows open. Now look at the place. Everything's sopping wet."

To add to the general wetness, Vanderbilt chose that time to shake himself, and for a moment the room was full of flying spray.

"Get that blasted hound out of here," Ralph snarled.

"Don't be so mean," Irene said, putting her arms around Vanderbilt's neck. "How can you send the poor little thing out into the storm?"

Vanderbilt rolled up his eyes, trying to look poor and little. Ralph snorted, and then snapped on an air conditioner that was set into one of the windows.

"All right, all right," he said. "At least we can cool the place off a little. It's so damp and hot in here, we're likely to die of tropical fever."

The Professor chuckled. "Well, if you don't mind," he said, "I'll just phone for a cab. It's urgent that I get home at once."

Danny stepped in front of him. "Wait, Professor," he said.

"But Dan, I can't wait—"

"I've been trying to tell you this," Danny said, in a rush. "It's no good your going home. The transmitter isn't there."

"Isn't there?" the Professor repeated, looking dazed. "I don't understand. Where is it?"

Unable to say another word, Danny pointed upward.

For an instant, the Professor lost his usual calm. "What?" he exploded. "Do you mean it's gone to heaven?"

"Just a moment," said Frank, stepping for-

ward. "Danny, is this transmitter you're talking about the one that went up on the plane?"

Danny nodded miserably.

"Up on a plane?" stammered the Professor.

"Good heavens!" said Frank. "Then you
mean it was a *real* transmitter—an invention
of the Professor's?"

"I hate to be stubborn," said Professor Bullfinch, "but I must insist that you tell me what
this is all about."

Rapidly, Frank explained how Snitcher had
tried to run off with the machine, and how the
loop of wire on the top of it had caught on the
wheel of the plane.

The Professor rubbed the top of his bald head
thoughtfully. "Dear me," he said. "This is
very awkward. How are we to get it down
safely?"

"Can't we go over to the control tower,"
Danny put in, "and have them get in touch
with the plane? They must have radio contact."

"Good idea," said Frank. "And we needn't
go over to the tower. We have an intercom
loud-speaker connection with them."

He led them into the adjoining office where,
on the desk, stood a large interoffice commu-
nicator. He switched it on and said, "George?
This is Frank Elswing."

They all heard the man in the tower say, "What's up, Frank?"

"Have you got a contact with that Tri-Pacer we have up there, seeding the clouds?"

"Yes, I have."

"Call him at once. It's urgent."

"Okay. Stand by."

They could all hear him quite clearly as he called the plane, and a few minutes later they heard the voice of Mr. Clark, distorted by a slight crackling, saying, "4257-Delta to tower. What is it, George?"

"Hold on, Abe," said the man in the tower.

And on the intercom he said, "What's your message, Frank?"

"Tell him he has a kid's wagon, with a machine attached to it, hanging from the axle of his right wheel."

Traffic control repeated the message. They

heard Clark say, "I thought we felt a little out of trim. That's going to make trouble when we land."

"Tell him the machine must not be harmed," the Professor put in.

When this had been told to Clark, he said, "I don't see how we're going to do it. We can't land without smashing up the machine. And we're going to have trouble just getting ourselves on the ground without an accident.''

The man in the tower said, ''How about getting a truck to drive along the strip, Abe, and you fly low at the same speed? Then somebody stands up in the bed of the truck, reaches up, and unhooks the machine from your wheel.''

''Oh, yes!'' Joe said. ''I saw that done on TV. It's easy!''

''Nothing doing,'' said Mr. Clark. ''I'm not a Hollywood stunt man. It's much too dangerous, especially for the man on the truck.''

There was a long, gloomy silence, which Ralph broke. ''The whole thing's impossible,'' he said.

The Professor sighed. ''You're right. Tell him to land his plane. Men are more important than machines.''

Mr. Elswing was turning to the intercom speaker, when Danny suddenly said, ''Wait. How do they throw the dry ice out of the plane?''

Frank raised an eyebrow at him. ''Why, they force open the door and just scatter it,'' he replied.

''Well,'' Danny said, ''is it possible that Mr. Clark could slow the plane down, and then maybe the copilot could step right out onto the wheel, reach down, and pull up the machine?''

The man in the tower had overheard this. ''I'll ask him,'' he said, and they heard him repeating Danny's idea to the pilot.

Then Clark said, ''Not a bad suggestion. I think we can do it that way, if the machine isn't too heavy. We'll try. If Harve drops it, watch your heads below.''

There was another silence that lasted for what seemed like hours. They all waited, holding their breaths as the minutes ticked away. And then, at last, Clark said, ''Two-five Delta to tower. We've got it, George.''

''Good!'' said Frank.

He snapped off the intercom, and they all looked at each other with relief. Ralph eyed Danny with something that almost resembled a smile, and said, ''That was pretty smart, boy. Where'd you learn so much about planes?''

''Professor Bullfinch taught me,'' answered Danny. ''Along with lots of other things.''

The Professor put a hand on Danny's shoulder. ''That's true, my boy,'' he said, in a gentle voice. ''And now, I think I may have to teach you something else. But first, suppose you tell me exactly what happened.''

17
Danny's Discovery Discovered

When Danny, with help from Irene and Joe, had finished his story, the Professor said nothing for several minutes. Deliberately, he took out his pipe, filled it, and lit it.

Then he said, "I have learned, in science, never to say that a thing is impossible. But what you tell me, Danny, is certainly very odd and very difficult to believe. It is possible, in theory, for the machine to work as you describe it—that is, for the very tiny particles to be chilled, and to have moisture condense in droplets around them, and for miniature clouds to form. I certainly didn't intend the transmitter to do such a thing, nor did I ever see it do so. I probably never used it under the necessary conditions, as you describe them. I'll withhold any decision until we have a chance to test it.''

''You can do that now, Professor,'' said Irene, who was standing near a window. ''Mr. Clark's plane just landed.''

''I'll be right back,'' said Danny. ''I'll go get IT.'' And off he dashed.

''Dear me, he certainly is hasty,'' said the Professor mildly. ''How can he get the plane?''

''He isn't going to get the plane, Professor Bullfinch,'' said Joe. ''He's going to get IT.''

''I'm afraid you are confusing me,'' murmured the Professor.

''*IT* is what we called the machine, for short,'' Irene explained. ''I.T. for ionic transmitter.''

In a very short time, Danny reappeared. Mr. Clark was helping him carry the machine. They set it down on the long table, and Clark nodded to the two meteorologists and the Professor.

''Congratulations, Abe,'' Frank said. ''I felt sure if you tried it again, the cloud-seeding would work.''

Clark blew out his lips. ''I wish it had,'' he replied. ''I like congratulations as much as anybody. Only it started to rain up there before we had a chance to throw out any more dry ice.''

''What?'' said Frank. ''But—then maybe it

rained as a result of your first trip up.''

"I doubt it." Clark shook his head. "I told you conditions weren't quite right. No, that's how the weather is: it just felt like raining, so it rained."

The Professor, who had been examining his machine, turned to Danny and said in a tense voice, "Dan, I want you to think carefully. This is important. When you got the transmitter from the plane, just now, was the switch on or off?"

Danny wrinkled his forehead. "It was on, Professor. I remember thinking that it must have closed when Vanderbilt was dragging Snitcher. I turned it off just before we brought it in."

"Aha!" Professor Bullfinch snapped his fingers. "I suspected as much. My dear boy, what you have here is a rain-making ray!"

All eyes were fastened on the Professor in astonishment.

Danny said in a bewildered tone, "But that's what I've been telling you, Professor. It makes little tiny rainstorms."

"No, Dan. It made the great big rainstorm which is still going on outside."

"That's impossible—" Ralph began.

"Tut, tut!" said the Professor, lifting a finger. "Not at all impossible. I believe that once the transmitter was up in the clouds, among all those droplets of water, it began making its own small clouds among the larger ones. Its drops grew heavy and began to fall. They carried others down with them. Sections of the larger cloud began to chill and condense also, and once this push had been given, the rain began in earnest.''

"But that machine doesn't work," Frank burst out. "I saw it for myself. Danny turned it on for me and nothing happened."

"Hmm." The Professor took his chin between thumb and forefinger. "Turn it on, Dan. Let's see."

Danny reached out and flipped the switch shut.

The rays shot out and met over the air conditioner. A dark-gray cloud, about the size of an armchair, formed in the air above the window. Suddenly small white particles began to whirl down. And the next minute, a blinding snowstorm filled the room.

"Hooray!" Joe yelled. "A white Christmas in August!"

The snowflakes settled in heaps on the table, on the teletype machine, on the map boards, on the instruments. They melted quickly, forming dirty pools of water.

The Professor quietly took out his handkerchief and put it over his bald head. "Very interesting," he remarked. "The cold air from the air-conditioner coils must be making this snow. A very instructive demonstration."

Frank had opened his umbrella and was trying to shield a pile of papers. Joe tried vainly to scoop up enough snow to make a snowball. Irene brushed snow from between Vanderbilt's ears.

As for Ralph, he was scowling more fiercely than ever. "Great guns!" he said. "If that blasted machine actually made the rain, and the cloud-seeding didn't—then I ate my new hat for nothing!"

Professor Bullfinch patted Danny's arm. "My boy," he said, "you have made a very useful discovery. In fact, I think the Academy may be more interested in the rain-making properties of the transmitter than in its other capabilities. However—"

Danny had been smiling broadly. At this, his smile vanished. "Yes, sir?" he said in a small voice.

"Here is the lesson I promised you earlier," the Professor said. "A scientist needs two qualities above all others: discipline and curiosity. He needs to be curious about how and

"A white Christmas in August."

why things work, and about their nature. He also needs to keep himself from jumping to conclusions, or from diving headlong into things without proper thought.

"Now, of those two qualities, you certainly have the curiosity. But you must also learn discipline."

He sighed. Then he went on, "And I'm afraid you will have to learn it the hard way. . . ."

18
The Hard Way

Slowly and steadily, back and forth along the floor of the weather station, Danny pushed the mop.

"Gosh," he said sadly, "there must be a simpler way to learn discipline than this."

Irene was helping him clean up the room. With a sponge, she blotted the slush from the surfaces of tables and instruments.

"Well, Dan, you must admit it's your own fault," she said.

"Yes, I know. Believe me, I'm going to stay away from sudden ideas from now on. And if I don't—" He looked about. On a hook near the door hung a brand-new panama hat, which Ralph Elswing had bought for himself to replace the other. "If I don't," Danny went on, "I'll eat Mr. Elswing's hat."

Irene spluttered with laughter. "Then I feel much safer," she said. "If Mr. Elswing ever caught you—"

"Caught him at what?" asked Joe, who entered the room at that moment. "What's he up to now?"

"Nothing. He just promised never to be headstrong again."

"Ha!" said Joe sarcastically. "This I have to see. Go ahead, Dan. Start in."

"Start in what?"

"Start in not getting crazy ideas."

Danny looked baffled. "How can you start in *not* doing something?"

"Oh, skip it," said Joe. "Look, I brought something for you."

"A new mop?" Danny said sourly.

"Come on, be serious. This is a present." Joe pulled a long sheet of paper out of his pocket. "A poem."

Joe was well known in school as a poet, and his verses, written for every occasion, were always applauded even if they were a bit strange.

Danny put down the mop. "That's nice of you, Joe," he said. "Go ahead. Read it."

Joe cleared his throat and began:

"Mark Twain made up a saying, and until now
  there was no reason to doubt it;
He said, 'Everybody talks about the weather but
  nobody does anything about it.'
Well, even though he is just a kid—
Danny Dunn did."

Irene uttered a shriek of laughter. "My goodness, Joe," she said. "What kind of English is that—'Danny done did'?"

Joe looked at her in surprise. "I didn't say, 'Danny done did.' I said. 'Danny Dunn did.' "

"Oh. I see, now," said Irene, with a wink at Danny. "I'm sorry I interrupted you. Please go on."

"Very well," said Joe, a little stiffly. "If you insist—

"He started with a tiny cloud,
Which made many grownups mad but it made his
  friends proud;
Then, just as a little acorn grows into a mighty
  oak,
The little rain cloud grew into a tremendous soak.

Now, even though what makes rainfall is still a
  mystery,
Danny's weather maker will go down in history.

"We might be able to make an ice-cream-soda cloud."

If he lived in France he would be on the President's
list
To be kissed on both cheeks as a fine scientist."

"Joe, it's a great poem!" Danny said, smiling affectionately at his friend.

"Thanks, Dan. It's for you."

"I appreciate it. And now, I have something for you."

"You have? What?"

"This." Danny thrust the mop into Joe's hands.

"Now, wait a minute," said Joe, backing away.

"Come on, Joe. You've got to help with the cleaning."

"But why? I'm not going to be a scientist. I'm going to be a writer."

"Writers need discipline, too," Danny said. "That's what Miss Arnold always tells us in English class. And this mess is partly your fault."

"Why is it my fault?"

"You should have stopped me. Go on. Mop."

Joe snorted, but he took the mop. He began working. After a moment, he glanced up. Danny was sitting on a dry part of the long table, with a pencil and paper, his face set in a frown of concentration.

"Hey!" said Joe. "Why aren't you mopping, too?"

"I'm figuring," Danny replied absent-mindedly. "If we bring the ray to the drugstore, and get Mr. Hopkins to leave the soda running and the tops off all the cans and syrup jars, we might be able to make an ice-cream-soda cloud. Then all we'd have to do is lie down with raincoats on—"

Irene put her hands on her hips, and looked sternly at him. Without another word, she marched over and got Mr. Elswing's hat down from the hook.

She strode to Danny's side, and held it out.

"Start eating," she said.

ABOUT THE AUTHORS
AND ILLUSTRATOR

JAY WILLIAMS has written over forty-five fiction and nonfiction books for children of all ages, in addition to coauthoring fifteen books about Danny Dunn. Mr. Williams was born in Buffalo, New York, and educated at the University of Pennsylvania, Columbia University, and the Art Students League.

RAYMOND ABRASHKIN wrote and coproduced the very popular and successful "Little Fugitive," a film that won an award at the Venice Film Festival.

EZRA JACK KEATS, Caldecott Award winner for *The Snowy Day,* has illustrated many children's books. He was born and raised in Brooklyn and studied at the Art Students League in New York City.